SHINGAS

D1198715

BARRY COLE

http://www.elbapublishing.co.uk

To Elizabeth

CONTENTS

PREFACE

The spoiling wine of war is spilled and soaked up once more by the earth and man's forgetfulness. Wolfe is dead and all England has wept. New France the reality and the dream is lost and the lily grows only in graveyards. Now fate stalks the forests and casts her spell. And so it begins again, more powerful than greed, progress without patience is an evil thing, it kills babies, the greatest sin but goes unpunished, it is not looked for when the murderer is sought. So history turns another page and waits with pen poised. Progress is impatient again and the children of the forest are doomed but first must come their war-cry.

ACKNOWLEDGMENTS

My thanks go to the following people: To my son, Paul, for his unstinting help and support. To Grant and Marika for creating the graphics and artwork for the cover. To Pauline for her faith and encouragement, and to Claire and Darren for proofing and editing the original manuscript.

CHAPTER ONE

T HE WAR WAS over. The bitter struggle which had seen the two great European nations of France and England locked in a bloody conflict for six years was ended. Now Canada together with all her dependencies had a new ruler; King George the third of England.

All that now remained was to take possession of those western outposts which still remained in French hands and this is where our story begins.

Fort Detroit November 1760.

From the quadrangle of firmed earth surrounded on each side by weathered palisades, Captain Beletre, the garrison commander, a stoutly built middle aged man, immaculately dressed in a three quarter length grey jacket, fixed his doleful gaze on the flag fluttering high above the ramparts. His aristocratic features, marred somewhat by a large aquiline nose, were fixed in a grim expression.

He had resolved to defend his post but when handed a copy of the capitulation by the English officer, together with a letter from the Marquis de Vaundreuil directing that the post should be given up without resistance, he had no choice but to surrender.

As his eyes settled on the billowing emblem of France, a shaft of sunlight pierced the cloud-filled November sky and for a brief moment, as though guided by some divine hand, its rays struck the eastern bastion of the fort, bathing it in a warm mellow light.

At that very moment a Grenadier, his scarlet coat embellished with the insignia of a corporal at arms, appeared on the timber battlement. Squinting in the unexpected brightness, he stepped forward, untied the rope at the foot of the flagstaff and began slowly lowering the Fleur De Lis.

Minutes later, and the corporal at arms took up the rope once more and accompanied by a rousing cheer from the detachment of English soldiers watching from outside the walls, he raised the blood red cross of St George aloft in its place.

Beletre lowered his gaze. As a soldier he felt the bitterness of defeat and as a Frenchman he felt the sadness of a lost land. But as a husband and a father, he was glad it was over; glad he was done with war.

For him, the moment of certainty had come two years earlier at Ticonderoga, when even as they perished in their hundreds on the French breastworks in a tempest of musket-balls, the heroism and determined valour displayed that day by the English soldiers showed a desire to wrest this land from whoever laid claim to it that was unstoppable. Pushing the bitter memory from his mind, Beletre turned to the warrior standing beside him, a Seneca war-chief and ally of the French and offered him a benign smile.

Shingas stared back at him with ink-black eyes. He was tall for his race, his body lean and muscular, his savage features emblazoned with war-paint. A single white heron's feather hung from his scalp-lock and suspended around his neck was a bear claw necklace. Every inch the warrior, his only clothing was a breech-cloth and thigh length leather leggings tied at the knee and deer-skin moccasins embellished with beads and porcupine quills. A knife and tomahawk hung from the belt around his waist. When he spoke, his French was imbued with the eloquence of his native tongue and although the language was foreign to him, learned over many hours from black robed Jesuits, his mastery of it was commendable.

'Why do you lay down your arms when we are many and they are few?'

'You think I don't want to fight?' Beletre replied, his face flushed with anger, his words imbued with bitterness.

Shingas, his face devoid of expression remained silent.

Beletre shrugged his shoulders. 'But I am forbidden. In France our Great Father has fallen asleep and while he slumbers he desires that we make peace with the English.'

'And what is to become of us? your brothers. Must we also make peace with these English dogs?'

'I must obey the wishes of my King and you must obey them also.'

'He is not my King.'

'That may be so but Shingas must know he cannot fight the English alone.'

'Shingas fought the Yenge before his French brothers took up arms against them. Shingas took many scalps and soon he will take many more.'

Overcome by a sense of sadness at Shingas' words and aware of the fate he knew awaited him and his people, Beletre paused for a moment, struggling inwardly to think of a way of conveying to this savage warrior the complex politics and intrigue of European statesmanship that had led to this moment. But he knew it was hopeless, it would be easier to make a length of rope out of sand and so instead, adopting a more conciliatory tone, he lied.

'Shingas is a great warrior but he must be patient, soon the Great Father will awaken and then he will send his armies to drive the English from the lands of his children.'

'The English King does not sleep and if Shingas does not fight, these dogs dressed in red will devour my people.'

Resigned to the hopelessness of further reasoning, Beletre touched a hand to his black gold trimmed tricorn hat, turned and walked away, contenting himself with thoughts of a return to the house he loved on the Rue St Antoine in Paris and a reunion with a family he had not seen for over five years. With both of his daughters now married, there was also the possibility of grandchildren to enjoy in his old age. But first there was the formality of surrender to attend to.

Ahead of him, flanked by two lines of redcoats the garrison of French soldier's, disarmed and dejected, filed out through the gates and marched along the dirt road leading down to the river and the waiting whale boats which would transport them across the stormy waters of Lake Eire and into captivity.

Off to one side, a large crowd of Pottawattamies and Wyandot warriors dressed in painted shirts and fluttering headdresses, looked on. Each of them amazed at this obsequious behaviour, and at a loss to understand why with so many men, the French troops should humble themselves before so few of their enemies.

With a gesture, Shingas gathered his war-party of twenty warriors around him and disarmed of their muskets and bullet sacks, they followed behind the grey-coated Troupes De La Marine as they left the sanctuary of the fort and trudged along the road towards the river.

Between the road and the forest the ground rose up forming a low hill and from this vantage point a young English officer observed proceedings with an indifferent air. Moments later his gaze fell upon Shingas and his warriors and immediately his persona changed. Turning away, he gestured urgently to a company of Redcoats taking their ease a short distance away. Obediently, with their muskets carried at the port, the soldiers jogged towards him.

Shingas caught the flurry of activity and watched as the company of soldiers gathered in a circle around the young Lieutenant like a pack of hunting hounds eager for the kill.

The young officer uttered an order and then striding out purposefully he set off down the slope towards the dirt road. A step behind him the grim faced soldiers formed up into two ranks and followed after him.

Shingas, his senses heightened, watched as they approached and what he saw filled him with dread; for unlike the rest of their comrades, the two soldiers bringing up the rear had their muskets slung over their shoulders and were carrying manacles and leg-irons.

With a guttural cry Shingas called out a warning and breaking into a run, he raced away across the cleared ground in front of the fort, a killing field for any attackers foolhardy enough to venture upon it. Heeding Shingas' cry, to a man the war-party chased after him, leaping over the stumps of the decapitated trees with the grace and agility of deer. With their hearts pounding they dashed towards the forest and safety.

Reaching the road, the company of Redcoats quickly formed up into two ranks, the front rank dropping down onto one knee while the second rank formed up a step behind them. Pausing for a moment to give each man time to raise his musket and select his target, the young officer then shouted out the order to fire.

The volley from the exploding muskets shattered the silence and droning like angry bees the musket balls flew among the fleeing war-party and six warriors fell to the ground with bloody holes in their backs. Spurred on, Shingas and the survivors raced headlong for the sanctuary of the trees.

Behind them, with practised precision, the soldiers reloaded their muskets, ramming wadding and ball home with their rods and then priming the musket pan with powder. When all were ready, the lieutenant called out his orders.

'Present! Fire!'

And once more the deafening crash of musket fire shattered the silence.

The fleeing Indians were almost at the tree-line when three warriors, lagging behind the others, were struck by the hail of lead balls and tumbled to the ground like skittles struck by a well thrown cheese.

The officer, his youthful cheeks flushed with colour, gave the order for his men to fix bayonets, then drawing his sword from its scabbard, he strode forward as though he was crossing a parade ground. Behind him with the naked steel of their bayonets glinting in the late morning sun, the soldiers formed a single line and advanced across the cleared ground, their heavy boots sinking into the soft mould.

Reaching the fallen Indians the soldiers moved from body to body and giving little thought as to whether they might be alive or dead, they stuck them with their bayonets, stabbing them again and again as though they were just lumps of meat. With the murderous work done and their once gleaming bayonets dripping with blood, they turned about and made their way back to the road.

Concealed by the dense foliage Shingas watched their butchery, his face devoid of expression. Taught from childhood to conceal all emotions, the lesson would not leave him but in his heart he swore a terrible revenge.

CHAPTER TWO

WITH ITS ONLY window shuttered, the small room was cloaked in almost total darkness, the only light allowed in was through the partially opened door. Standing beside it was Saul, a tall well-built man in his mid-twenties his handsome features framed by a mane of dark brown shoulder length hair. Wearing nothing except for a pair of breeches held up by a leather strap, he pressed his ear against the opening, straining to catch the sound coming from the adjoining room, a man's voice but so quiet he could barely hear it.

Oblong in shape the adjoining room was sparsely furnished and being the cabins largest room, it served both as kitchen and sitting room with a curtained off area in the far corner, behind which was a small bed. A ten-foot table-board set on trestles and surrounded by six chairs dominated the centre of the room. Set in the far wall was a solid door secured by two metal bolts with a narrow window on either side of it, each covered by a wooden shutter. A stone fireplace housing a large cast iron stove, occupied much of the longest wall, its dying fire bathing the room in a soft orange glow.

Seated at either end of the table were two people; their faces illuminated by the light from a glass sided lantern suspended above them on a hook driven into a roof beam. The only sound to intrude upon the silence was the rhythmic ticking of a brass-crowned clock, resting on the mantel-shelf above the fireplace.

Samuel Endicote, a broad shouldered man in his sixties with a weathered face and close cropped greying hair looked across at the woman facing him, his small bright eyes staring into her face, expectantly.

Esther held his gaze for a moment then lowered her eyes, focusing them on Samuel's calloused hands, a farmer's hands, placed palms down on the table in front of him. His words had unsettled her and even as her thoughts flitted between doubts and possibilities, overshadowing both was a sense of disbelief; could he really wish this of her? When he spoke again, the sound of his voice, although not loud, startled her.

'Well have you no answer for me?'

Esther sensed the impatience in his tone but she waited a moment longer before replying.

'You... You wish me to marry Adam?'

'Yes and in exchange you shall have your freedom and more besides.'

Esther felt her heartbeat quicken, could this be possible, a simple yes and she would be free of her indenture? But before she could utter the word, others spilled uninvited from her mouth.

'But Adam is... He is,'

'A child! A simpleton!' Samuel spat out the words as though they were bile.

Esther averted her eyes, vexed at her stupid outburst.

Clenching his fists, Samuel leaned forward, his lips curled into a salacious grin.

'That he may be but for all that he is still a man.'

Esther, shocked by what the words implied, lifted a hand to her mouth. Pleased with the effect his words had evoked, Samuel glared at her for a moment then settling back in his chair he allowed his anger to dissipate before continuing in a softer tone.

'But that is not the reason for what I propose.' Then pausing for a moment as if to gather his thoughts, he went on. 'As our first born Adam will inherit this farm but how long do you suppose before his brother Saul steals it away from him? Answer me that?'

Her composure restored, Esther remained silent, letting him continue.

'Oh I know my sons well and Saul would do it I have no doubt of that. But I also know you mistress Colwill and it is my belief that if you were Adam's wife then he'd surely not succeed.'

Esther met his gaze, surer now of her position and in the possibilities the matter at hand offered her.

'So, what say you, will you do it? Will you wed Adam?'

'And I should be freed of my indenture?'

Samuel allowed the smallest of smiles to soften his face.

'Of course child. I may only be a farmer but I cannot have a son of mine wedded to a servant.'

'And be mistress in my own right?'

'You have my word on it.'

Esther pondered for a moment. Her mind was made up but it would do no harm for him to wait on her reply. Finally, taking a deep breath she gave him her decision.

'Then I will agree to it, I will do what you ask.'

Turning away from the door, Saul pushed it shut. He had heard everything but rather than scowling, it was a smile which showed on his face. With practised ease he padded across the darkened room and down the narrow aisle between the two beds which took up much of the space.

Pausing for a moment he gazed down at the faint outline of Kit his youngest brother, his head buried in a pillow, lost in sleep, his small hand clutching a corner of the blanket pulled up around his shoulders as though fearful that someone would snatch it away from him. From the bed opposite, the heavy breathing of his other two brothers told him that neither were aware of him eaves dropping.

Soundlessly, Saul lowered himself onto the bed beside Kit and stretched out, his hands locked behind his head. Although he was tired, the prospect of something other than sleep kept him awake.

Minutes passed and in the silence of the darkened room the faint striking of the mantel clock was like the clanging of a steeple bell in his head. Careful not to disturb Kit, Saul got up from the bed and navigating his way to the door, he opened it and slipped outside into the adjoining room.

The fire still burned in the stove and together with the sallow light from a single candle, its warm glow infiltrated the darkness and gave substance to the table and chairs and to the heavy curtain suspended from the ceiling, giving privacy to the space hidden behind it.

His bare feet soundless on the wooden floor, Saul crossed to the curtain and grasping one end with his hand he drew it aside to reveal a narrow bed pushed up against the wall and lying in it was Esther.

Stretched out on the bed, resting on one elbow, her body covered by a patterned quilt, Esther gazed up at him, her grey-blue eyes glistening like jewels in the guttering candle-light. She was not surprised to see him, for she had known he would come, just as surely as she had known he would be listening to all that was said between her and his father. An inviting smile played at the corners of her full mouth and with the grace of Salome she drew aside the blanket and revealed herself to him.

She wore a simple full length cotton nightdress provocatively opened at the neck to expose the soft valley between her breasts. Stepping closer to the bed Saul gazed down at her, his heart thumping with desire. Esther's smile widened seductively and reaching down she grasped the hem of her nightgown and pulled it tantalisingly up over her thighs. For the briefest of moments

Saul devoured her with his eyes, then pulling at the cord around his waist he let his breeches drop down around his ankles.

Esther stared up at his naked body, then reaching out her hand she gripped his arm and pulled him down onto the bed beside her. His throat dry with passion, Saul gripped her shoulders in a vice-like grip and pushed her down onto the bed. Arching her neck, Esther stared up at him her eyes smouldering, her lips full and inviting. With a half suppressed cry Saul covered her with his mouth, his lips crushing hers. Esther moaned softly and enfolded him in her arms, drawing him into her, feeling his naked chest crushing her breasts. Freeing his arm Saul reached his hand down between her thighs and forced them apart, his fingers searching for her womanhood in the silky triangle of pubic hair, his heart racing when he heard her groan with pleasure as he caressed the velvety softness of her secret wound.

Inflamed by his touch, Esther gripped his arm and pulling his hand away she spread her legs, wrapping them tightly around him, encircling his waist with her naked thighs and pulling him into her. With the cloying scent of her musk clogging his nostrils, consumed with lust, Saul plunged into her, feeling her body arching as he thrust into her, again and again in an ever quickening rhythm, her wide child-bearing hips pushing upwards, meeting his thrusts with her own, her nails clawing his naked back and bloodying it with deep scratches.

In moments it was over and spent, Saul rolled off her and lay on his back panting, his body glistening with sweat. With a pretence at modesty, Esther pulled down her nightdress and rolled onto her side to face him, staring into his handsome face, letting her gaze wash over his features, his dark liquid eyes, the perfect line of his jaw. She knew there was no love between them, just a need, a hunger for each other's bodies. But it suited them both and she was always mindful to only let him get between her legs when she knew it was safe for her to do so. Illicit though it was, their love-making gave her much pleasure and also made the hardships of her life more bearable.

Pondering on this, Esther was suddenly aware of the momentous consequences that the events of the evening would have on her life and what this marriage to Adam would truly mean for her. Lifting her eyes away from her lover's face, for the first time in all her years of servitude, of being passed from family to family like a chattel since she was sixteen, she experienced a moment of utter contentment.

CHAPTER THREE

THERE WERE SEVEN of them; each dressed in a greasy hunting frock of smoked deer-skin with horse-hair fringes. A rough and truculent bunch with stubble chins and lank shoulder length hair tucked under caps of varying styles, some cut from felt and stuck with feathers, others fashioned from the skin of beaver or otter. Hardy men, brought together without a care for their compatibility. It was enough that each of them hated work as much as they did Indians but would suffer a little of both for the pure perils of the life and its fickle rewards.

Two weeks earlier five of them had left the frontier city of Albany with its busy wharfs and narrow streets crowded with families seeking a new life in the vast wilderness beyond. In a hired bateau, crewed by three men with knowledge of the river and heavily loaded with every possible artefact of trade including six quarter barrels of raw whiskey, they had rowed up the Mohawk river. On passed the old Dutchman's town of Schenectady with its pretty houses and waving children, then around the long bend to Fort Hunter at the mouth of the Schoharie River. With a 'hello' to the sentries as they passed beneath its tall ramparts, they bent their backs until they reached Fort Herkimer at the German flats and the welcome offer of board and lodgings for the night.

Dawn saw them on their way once more and after a weary pull against a current which had caught a scent of the sea, they reached Fort Stanwix and the head of the river navigation. Here the bateau was unloaded and the goods put inside the walls for the night and for men better used to a less arduous life, a welcome bed.

By early next morning all of the trade goods, save for ten muskets, confiscated by the fort's commander for no other reason than to ensure that they should not be traded to capricious savages who would later use them against his majesty's subjects, were loaded onto the backs of sixteen pack-horses. With the bateau sent back down river, the five men and the pack train passed through the fort gates and began their journey westward to Wood Creek, a wild and rushing stream bordered by towering elms and ageless oaks. After almost losing two of their animals fording the deep waters of the creek, the pack train continued on into the dark recesses of the spruce woods beyond. They were on familiar ground now and after twenty more hard miles they at last reached their destination. Long abandoned by the military, the little wooden fortress of Royal Blockhouse was situated at the eastern end of Oneida Lake. With i its leaky roof and crumbling walls, it was now the home of an old settler who resided there together with his two milk cows and several racoons. Due in part to his rheumaticky legs, the old man confined his camp-hawking to a village of Oneida Indians on the opposite shore and then only from necessity. However the pack-train with its wealth of trade goods was not destined for his miserable storeroom but instead for the warehouse of Thomas Gann who, favouring its location above its regal name, had chosen the spot as his headquarters. A bold and forward looking man, at the conclusion of the war with the French, he had turned his energies towards the profitable though often precarious business of fur trading, where rivalry among the various traders was fierce and murder was commonplace. But for all that, great profits rewarded the successful, and Gann, whose character combined the astuteness of a banker with the morality of a highwayman, was not a man to be unsuccessful.

And so it was, that due to his quick mind and greedy fingers, the seven men and their pack-horses now found themselves venturing into the heart of the Genessee valley, the home of the Seneca.

For three days they travelled through the primeval forest with its scaly towers, tangled thickets and pine swamps. Although a June sun burned in the sky above, beneath the endless canopy all was shade and shadow. Only the sun's warmth penetrated the verdure, where it hung like an invisible mist heavy with the pungent perfume of resin and decay.

With day and night colliding, they emerged from the gloomy depths and made their way along the margin of a narrow lake, its surface shimmering in the late afternoon sun as though it were covered by a million golden pennies. A weariness of body betrayed itself in the men's rugged faces and in the dull, dark eyes of the horses. So all were relieved when reaching a narrow strand at the western end of the lake, Quinty Soule the brigade's leader, called a halt. All around them thickly wooded hills ran down to reflect upon the water but here lake and land met on a level and the forest was held back by a narrow meadow of pale grass, flanked by white birch and alders.

Flute, a short, stocky man in his forties with the face of a jovial innkeeper, untied a sack from one of the horses and tipping it up, emptied an assortment of blackened pots and pans onto the ground. This simple act singled him out as the cook and while his only qualification for the work was nothing more than his willingness to undertake the task. The others, as much from laziness as anything else, accepted his role even though they knew that on occasions his culinary efforts would inflict upon them bouts of diarrhoea.

Without the need for orders, Blessing, a bear of a man with short stocky legs, powerful arms and a barrel chest and a lanky youth named Linnet, his smallpox scarred face framed by long straggly hair, moved away towards the tree line and began gathering firewood. The remaining traders set about unloading the bundles of trade goods from the backs of the horses and stacking them in orderly piles on the ground.

Unburdened, the horses were led away and tethered securely by their halters to a length of rope strung between two trees. Seeing them settled, Doublejohn, the brigade's appointed horse-minder, moved along the line and dipping a hand into the gunny sack he was carrying, fed each of them a handful of corn.

With darkness closing in Blessing and Linnet returned, their arms laden with firewood and within minutes they had a fire lit, its welcome glow attracting the others to it like moths to a candle. McCallum, a wiry built man with narrow shoulders and wearing a cap resembling a tam-o-shanter made from a scrap of tartan cloth, set an animal skin bundle down on the ground and running his tongue over his thin lips, he pulled back the flaps to reveal a haunch of venison.

In an instant, Flute had it skewered on a rusty iron pole, kept among his utensils for just such a purpose and after basting the purple flesh in a glutinous substance, resembling axle grease, he rested the pole in the notched ends of two sticks set on opposite sides of the fire.

With their appetites whetted, the ring of traders edged closer to the fire, their eyes fixed greedily on the haunch of venison spitting and sizzled in the flames embrace. But even as the seven traders watched their supper cooking, other eyes were watching them.

The four Seneca warriors were well hidden by the dense branches of spruce, their copper coloured skin encouraging concealment. Each was naked except for a breech-cloth and thigh-length leggings, their heads were naked also, shaved clean but for a single lock of hair, at the crown. All were armed with a tomahawk and a flintlock musket. They had followed the pack-trains progress through the forest and watched unseen as the traders made camp.

'They are Yenge traders. We will speak with them.'

The warrior who spoke was named Pahotan, his voice kept low, his words softly spoken. He was the eldest of the party and their leader. The other three warriors remained silent, they were young men and they had not been asked for their judgement. His decision made, Pahotan climbed to his feet and accompanied by one of the young warriors, he slipped away into the surrounding trees.

It was Doublejohn who saw them first. He had taken the last two horses down to the water's edge to drink and while they stood in the shallows slaking their thirst, he busied himself washing their legs. Dipping a handful of grass into the water and then running it down their legs from knee to hoof. All of the horses had been scratched by the hard-beaked thorns of briar bushes and while none of the wounds were deep, in the morning these cuts would prove irresistible to the forest's flies. The youngest of the mares was the last to be washed and although he handled her gently, she became skittish and tap-stepped away from him, nostrils flared, her neat ears laid back. Throwing down the handful of wet grass, Doublejohn soothed her with his voice and pulling gently on the mare's halter rope he brought her under control.

Using his hands to wash off the last of the blood from her cuts, satisfied, Doublejohn turned his back on the lake and lead the two horses out of the shallows. In that moment he saw the two Indians emerge from the tree-line and walk towards the traders' camp. Even without war-paint they exuded an aura of menace.

For a brief moment a look of concern clouded his face but when he spoke his voice was calm, his accent pure Cornish.

'Look to, we haz us zum company.'

Alerted, the men seated around the cooking fire reached for their muskets and turned to face the supposed danger.

'Steady lads I don't think they mean us harm.'

It was Soule who spoke and setting down his musket he climbed to his feet and walked slowly towards where Pahotan and the young warrior stood motionless at a distance which, while showing their boldness, also gave them a good chance of escape should the Yenge prove unfriendly.

Although not a tall man, Soule's upright bearing made him appear so and with a deer-skin shirt worn over scarlet leggings and his long greasy black hair tied back in a single braid, he epitomised the breed of men called Coureurs de bois by the French. His weathered features were marred by a purple welt which ran from eye socket to jaw, a testament to the perils of the life.

Watching from the camp, none heard what was spoken but all were relieved when Soule turned and led the two Indians back to the fire, calling out as he approached them.

'We've had us a stroke of luck boys, this pair are Seneca and they say they will guide us to their village.'

'Meat will burn if it's not eaten.'

It was Ben Flute who spoke up, reminding all that they had stomachs in need of filling. Immediately all found a place at the fire and without a thought for manners, each man quickly tore or cut a helping from the roasted meat and stuffed it into his mouth until it overflowed at the corners like a burst sack.

After wiping his sleeve across his greasy mouth, Flute lifted a large blackened kettle off the fire and with unerring aim, splashed scalding hot coffee into three large tin cups all of which carried dents but as yet had not sprung a leak. As captain, Soule had one to himself, the remaining pair were passed from lip to lip until they were drained and then topped up again until the kettle was empty.

A chorus of hearty belches marked the meal's conclusion and each man dipped into his pocket and took out his pipe and tobacco and lit them with a stick from the fire. Soon clouds of sweet scented smoke filled the air, a delight to the nostrils and good proof against the blood sucking insects which plagued the water's edge.

Presently, Bailey, a thin faced man with a sensitive nose and mournful eyes, took a pair of dice, carved from bone from the bullet sack suspended around his neck and a game was begun much to the delight of the two Seneca warriors who eagerly dipped their greasy fingers into their shot pouches for the bet.

Soule sat apart from the others, looking over his cup at the loose circle of players across the fire, his gaze lingering on the two Indians. Each had a tomahawk in his belt and a scalping knife carried in a high necked sheath decorated with coloured quills. A leather satchel, a carry-all and a powder-horn hung from straps coming over the shoulder and across the chest, resting easy on their hip. Before his interest fell away, Soule's eyes focused on their rifles. They were military flintlocks, the type given by the English to their Indians allies but such was the capricious nature of the race that he took little comfort in the fact. The older warrior had told him that his people would welcome the trade goods they brought and he had no reason to doubt him. If the pair were up to bad tricks they would find out soon enough and knowing that the men he travelled with, even young Linnet, were used to such dangers gave him some comfort.

As the evening passed into night the game was abandoned and finding a space around the dying fire, the players stretched out on the ground and were soon asleep, their snores and heavy breathing a testament to the arduous rigours of the day and bellies full of venison.

Unable to settle, Soule threw some wood on the fire and warmed his cup from the dregs left in the kettle. From the lake, lost now in inky blackness, the melancholy notes of a loon were snatched up and scattered among the treetops by a wind going nowhere.

CHAPTER FOUR

F LUTE WAS THE first of them to crawl from his blanket. And even before men with sleepy eyes yawned themselves awake he had a fire lit and a kettle boiling before they crowded around his fire complaining at the lateness of the meal.

For all of them, breakfast was the cold remains of the supper's meat, washed down with cups of scalding coffee. A dozen or so journey cakes lay warming on a skillet over the fire, and those hungry enough to ignore the mould wolfed them down.

The first to finish his meal, Doublejohn freed the horses of their hobbles and led them into camp to be burdened once more with their heavy packs. Willing hands lent themselves to the task, while Doublejohn, mindful of the horses' welfare, checked their girth straps, that none were too tight or too slack.

Flute put his pots and pans into a greasy gunny-sack, with nothing washed or wiped, it took but a moment. The remains of the coffee he splashed on the fire, then pulling open the front of his breeches he took out his flaccid cock and with commendable dexterity, extinguished the remaining flames by urinating on them.

With the morning sun climbing into the sky, pale and yellow as the yoke of an egg and with Doublejohn finished fussing over his horses, Soule shouted out.

'All's ready, let's be gone.'

At the sound of his voice, Pahotan and the young warrior, their rifles cradled in the crook of their arm, turned their faces southwards and walked purposefully towards the encircling forest.

Pulling sharply on the halter rope of the lead horse Blessing followed after them. Behind him, strung out in single file, the brigade followed, each man eager to be on his way.

Hidden from view, the two young Seneca warriors watched as the brigade was swallowed up by the wall of trees and when the last horse had disappeared from sight, they turned their backs on the lake and melted away unseen into the dark-green bosom of the forest.

All morning the brigade moved deeper into the primeval forest, the scaly trunks of its trees towering over them, dark and foreboding. Occasionally a shaft of golden sunlight would pierce the dense canopy and lift their spirits, while the smells of must and mould clogged their nostrils and the enduring silence preyed on their senses.

Thankfully as they neared the Genessee River the forest became noticeably fresher and towering hemlocks gave way to elms and oaks and as daylight filtered through their spreading branches the woods took on new colours.

Two hours before midday, as men and horses splashed across a wide stream, its banks thick with bayberries and ground-vine, their nostrils caught the redolent smell of wood smoke carried in on a cooling breeze. Heartened, they forded the stream and climbed the low hill beyond. When all were gathered at the crest, Pahotan pointed towards a hillside planted with rows of squash and maize. Just beyond them were the distinctive elm bark long-houses of the Iroquois. Turning to Soule he said with a note of pride in his voice.

'Tiataroga.' This was his village, they had reached their destination.

Moments later, as if by magic, a crowd of noisy, naked children with small black mischievous eyes, came scampering pell-mell down the hill towards them shouting with excitement and waving their skinny arms like the sails of a windmill. Several of the older girls carried a baby on their hip, grinning and bubbling at their bouncy outing. Following on their heels were a pack of lean wolfish camp-dogs the hair on their necks bristling, their snarls and barks adding to the din.

Many of these mischiefs had never seen a horse before but none were overawed and several of them took great delight in running up and touching them with their hand and then scampering away shrieking with excitement. Some even thought it a great game to duck beneath the bellies of the horses and race away whooping at their bravery. To the dogs however, the horses were four legs to be snapped at and bitten. That was until Doublejohn swung his foot and caught two of them with the toe of his boot, sending them scampering away with their tails between their legs.

Not known for his conviviality, Bailey surprised all by scooping up child after child in his strong arms and setting them up onto a horse. Soon each animal had a terrified rider astride its neck, clutching handfuls of mane and clinging on with skinny legs.

'See how they loves it John-John. See how they loves it.'

There was no doubting that he meant the horses and so with a half-smile Doublejohn let the intended rebuke die on his lips.

Oblivious to it all, Pahotan strode away along a narrow path towards the village. The fur-traders followed and no sooner had they reached the outlying long-houses when they were immediately surrounded by a swarm of squaws in their all-alike doeskin dress, chattering excitedly in high pitched voices and craning their necks for a good view of these English traders, each eager to know what trinkets and baubles they carried in their packs.

Without exception, the men, mostly warriors, kept to the fringe of the crowd, haughty and aloof, looking on with measured indifference. They had been told in detail about the men who now came amongst them by the two young warriors when they returned to the village. They knew each of these Yenge traders as if they had seen them with their own eyes.

Now with their lithe bodies glistening with sweat, the two young warriors paused for a moment at the entrance to the council-house, then pulling aside the curtain they slipped inside.

The gloomy building was lit by a few tallow candles, their feeble light reflecting off its elm bark walls, each section secured by upright wooden stakes. The building's arched roof, blackened by smoke from countless fires, was supported down its spline by rows of stout wooden posts set at regular intervals along its length. At the centre a large smoke hole allow in some light, which pooled in a yellowish circle onto the rush mat flooring.

Seated beneath it on a low bench fronted by a shallow pit containing the flickering remnants of a fire, were several tribal elders, old men, their keen deep set eyes gleaming in their sockets, their stern features betraying little emotion. Each wore a gaudy blanket draped over his naked shoulders, their necks adorned with necklaces and amulets fashioned from the claws of wild animals and the bones of small birds.

Standing before them beyond the fire, was Kiashuta a chief from a neighbouring tribe, his bold features daubed in ochre and soot, his head shaven down both sides with a mane of hair reaching down to his broad shoulders. Hung around his neck was a silver gorget, a trophy looted from the body of a dead English officer. Grouped around him were three other warriors, their faces streaked with war-paint and each armed with either a tomahawk or a war-club. When he spoke his voice was strong, his words emotive.

Pausing in his address Kiashuta took a cloth bundle from one of his cohorts and with a dramatic flourish he unfolded it to reveal a wampum belt crafted from purple and black shells and in its folds, a blood stained tomahawk. With a loud war-whoop he took hold of the tomahawk and flung it down at the feet of the elders.

A heavy silence hung in the air, then slowly Wapontak, the principal elder rose from the bench and stepped forward into a shaft of sunlight, which held him like a spotlight. A tall man with bold, crafty features, he wore a trade blanket across one shoulder and his thigh length leggings were embellished with the scalps of his enemies. A scalping-knife and hatchet hung from the belt around his waist. Expressionless he stood for a moment looking down at the bloody axe and then in one fluid movement he pulled off his blanket and threw it over the axe, covering it and in a rising voice he addressed the warriors standing before him.

'Do you think us fools that we would believe your lies? These French you speak of are far, away and growing smaller and the English have their foot upon their neck. Can they give my people blankets, kettles, gunpowder and shot? No, only the English can give us these things and yet you would have us take up the hatchet against them. I say go away from us now before the anger in my heart swallows you up.'

Seething with rage Kiashuta threw down the war-belt and whirling about he strode away towards the doorway. Immediately, one of his emissaries snatched up the tokens and together with the two other warriors he followed after his chief. Pausing in the doorway, the one carrying the war-tokens turned and for a brief moment stared at Wapontak, his face, disfigured by a patch of scar tissue where flames had burned away the flesh, twisted into a malevolent mask. Then snatching aside the curtain he turned and was gone.

Eager to impart their news the two young Seneca warriors stepped forward and addressed the elders. Lurking in the shadows, a silent spectator, their words carried to Shingas and instantly his invidious mind seized on the hope that the arrival of these fur-traders may somehow offer him a chance to restore his reputation and standing as a war-chief, lost to him by the calamitous death of so many of his warriors at Detroit.

Outside, enveloped now by the entourage of excited Seneca, Pahotan led the fur-traders and their pack-horses through the village and into the quadrangle at its centre, a large square of ground as much as half an acre in area and enclosed on three sides by orderly rows of long-houses. The only tenants of this dry patch of ground were what appeared at first sight to be tree trunks, grouped in a triangle with ten or so yards separating one from the other. Their height had been ordained by an axe some eight feet above their roots and their trunks were so burned and charred by the flames of unnumbered fires as to be unrecognisable. They were burning posts at which, horrors of pain too terrible to detail or recount were suffered by those unfortunate enough to have their fate decided by the capricious minds of their captors.

Beyond the trilogy of blackened stakes, two warriors emerged from the council-house carrying a long wooden bench, which they placed in the middle of the quadrangle a few feet away from where a mat woven from rushes had been spread out on the ground. Moments later Wapontak stepped out into the sunlight and followed by the tribal elders, he walked over to the bench and seated himself at its centre leaving the other old men to find room for themselves alongside him. Theirs was the status of age, experience was their wisdom and they were honoured above the fiercest warrior. The flowers of their seed were all about them, the young warriors the mirrors on their memory, their people their only concern. As they seated themselves, a party of warriors, each armed with a hatchet and musket, gathered about them like a guard of honour.

With Pahotan at its head, the unruly procession, crowded onto the quadrangle and as if by magic, a quietness settled over the gathering, even babies were hushed or given their thumb to suck on. All noise subsided and an expectant hush settled over the assembly, nothing intruded on the silence, not even the yapping of a dog.

Soule, ever watchful, followed Pahotan with his eyes as their guide approached Wapontak and spoke into his ear. Turning away the old sachem said something and immediately a warrior strode across to the council house and slipped inside. Moments later the same warrior emerged holding a lighted pipe, its long stem adorned with the wing feathers of a jay. Walking across to Wapontak he placed it into the old chief's outstretched hands. Taking his cue, Soule walked forward and seated himself cross-legged on the rush mat.

Wapontak brought the calumet with its carved stone bowl to his lips and drew the smoke from the sweet scented tobacco into his mouth. Exhaling, he passed the pipe to the man seated on his left. And so it continued until all the elders had taken a smoke and the calumet passed back to Wapontak. For a moment Wapontak held the pipe aloft, his eyes staring into the sky, then reached out his arms he passed it to Soule. Taking the proffered pipe, Soule put it to his lips and took in a mouthful of smoke then, passing it back to the Seneca sachem, he turned and beckoned to Bailey.

Aware of his role, Bailey approached one of the horses and pulling a small bundle of blue cloth tied up with a short length of rope from one of the packs, he carried it over to him. Untying the rope and with great panache Soule unfurled the bundle corner by corner to reveal its contents; two bone handled knifes, twists of tobacco, leather pouches filled with paint powder, a different colour in each and a string of purple shells.

Wapontak ran his eyes over the gifts and he was pleased. Taking the calumet in his hands he held it aloft and in a strong voice he addressed the traders, speaking in the dialect of his people, knowing that at least one among the Yenge would understand his words.

'You are come at last Englishmen and I welcome you. In the forest of the Onondowaga you are strangers but we welcome you, for you are the good men among your people, I will not speak of the ones who anger me.'

Soule climbed slowly to his feet and stood a moment looking around at the sea of faces surrounding him before replying. When he spoke he did so with confidence, timidity he knew would be seen as a weakness by these people and given their capricious nature he knew full well that it was best to appear resolute and purposeful in all matters.

'We are glad of your welcome. It is true we are strangers but we have left our footprints in the forest so that we may find our way again. We have walked far, from the shores of Oneida Lake, our legs are weary but we are glad.'

Murmurs of approval rippled through the crowd. Soule paused for a moment, he was beginning to enjoy himself and when he spoke again his voice had a more serious tone to it.

'I know there have been Frenchmen here.'

This was a guess as his only evidence was that the two who had guided them had used French shot from their pouches to gamble with the previous evening.

He paused, waited for the murmurings of discontent among the crowd to die down before continuing.

'But I am pleased that you have closed your ears to their lies and welcome us as brothers. These French are jealous of our great friendship, they would lie and spread false tales then cheat you of your furs. We bring you good trade, we still hold tightly to the chain of friendship that the Iroquois and the English have long held, not once has it fallen from our hands.'

Wapontak listened intently his eyes fixed on Soule as he spoke. He was surprised that they knew that Frenchmen had been in his village but he was sure that they spoke of a less recent time. More than this he was angered by the man's hollow words. The chain of friendship of which he spoke was little more than words on the tongue. These English walked with a broad and heavy foot upon the lands of the Iroquois and the officers and soldiers of the forts within the boundary of their lands treated them with contempt and abuse. There were already those among the Seneca who talked of war against the English before it was too late and before they themselves like the French were 'kicked out of the way'. And these bad Frenchmen of whom the Yenge spoke had brought guns and blankets to his village in the winter. They had been a help to his people when the English with-held their customary presents to his people, caring little that having come to rely on them for their existence, that they must suffer when deprived of them. It was true these 'Coureurs de bois' also came with intentions of speaking against the English, seeking to incite his warriors against them. Telling how the English would neglect them, steal their lands and finally destroy them unless they and all the tribes of the Iroquois nation rose up against them and urged that the guns they had brought be used against them before all was lost. Wapontak saw how these seeds planted with malice began to grow as truth but he also saw the laden pack-horses and remembered first the needs of his people. When he spoke his voice was firm, his words carefully chosen.

'Our ears listen to your promises, your words are welcome but among us promises must be seen with the eye and only then can they be believed.'

A murmur hurried through the crowd and in an instant Soule was moving among the pack-horses talking in a raised voice as he sent his hands patting the packs in time with his words.

'See we bring you powder and shot, warm blankets, fine sharp knives, hatchets, red cloth, tobacco, good whiskey to wet your throats, hawks-bells and beads.'

No sooner had Soule fallen silent when an elder, his thin body wrapped in a red blanket pointed at him and spoke out in a reedy voice, his words an accusation.

'You bring us no guns.'

The words sent a shiver down Soule's spine but he was prepared and turning on his heels he called out to Flute.

'Bring me your cups and fetch down one of the barrels. Quickly now.' Then with arms held aloft he turned to face his accuser.

'Hear me! Among these woods are those who would kill us. Those who send out the war-belt do not tell us their names. Should we bring guns to those who would kill us?'

The elders turned their gaze on Red Blanket angered that he had spoken out.

Soule called out again, raising his voice so all would hear.

'Wait there is more! We do not know your villages, we do not know who lights the welcome fire and who instead lights fires to burn us in. Are we fools who would bring guns to those who could be our enemies and hold them out saying kill me? No first we must see the faces of our true brothers, only then can we give them guns to fight their enemies.'

Even as Soule spoke Flute had the bung out of one of the barrels and was already splashing the raw whiskey into the three tin cups, before pushing them into the outstretched hands of Wapontak and two other elders.

Putting the cup to his lips, Wapontak drank deeply. The fiery liquid caused a mist to come into his eyes and scorched his throat but still he took a second swig before passing the half empty cup to the elder seated next to him. At last the cup reached Red Blanket and after draining what remained of the liquor in a single swallow he offered the cup for more. Reluctantly, Flute took it from his clutching fingers and slopped it to the brim with whiskey. Better he reasoned to see the old fool drunk than have him cause more trouble.

Satisfied, Wapontak rose to his feet and in a rising voice he addressed the assembled tribe.

'My people these Englishmen have come among us with much to trade. Go now and bring out the fruits of your winter hunt, show them what great hunters you are. Also let fires be lit so that they may fill their bellies and know that the Onondowaga are still their brothers and that the ancient chain of friendship is still held tightly in our hands.'

Immediately a great shout went up from the crowd and even before his words had died away they were already dispersing, running in all directions whooping and yelling like children let out from school.

Just as quickly but in a more ordered fashion, Soule and his men began stripping the horses of their heavy packs and after spreading a line of blankets on the ground, they began laying out the trade goods upon them. Each man would take a share of the profits so care was taken by all to display each item, whether a string of beads or a blanket, in such a way that it would tempt even the most reticent buyer into parting with his furs.

With the horse freed of their packs, surrounded by a troop of mischievous children, Doublejohn led them away beyond the encircling long-houses to a grassy spot where earlier he had secured a tethering rope between the trunks of two trees. Tying up each of the horses by their halter reign, he took up a half empty sack of oats and walking along the line, shook out a helping of provender for each animal. Happy that they were settled, Doublejohn and his entourage of black-eyed imps made their way back to the quadrangle. He had let the horses drink their fill from the stream as they entered the village so they would last till sunset before needing to quench their thirst.

When all was laid out to Soule's satisfaction, he put Flute and Linnet in charge of the three barrels of whiskey. Anticipating early customers, the pair soon had the lid off one of the barrels and stood beside it, each with a tin cup in their hand ready to ladle out a measure of the 'fire-water' in exchange for a beaver pelt or some other exquisite fur.

Gripped with excitement, her pretty face radiant with bear's oil and vermilion, Minawa wove her way through the throng of people. Heavy with child, she moved slowly, her doe-skin dress, beautifully decorated with coloured beads and small shells stretched tight across her distended abdomen. She had never before seen a white man and certainly never set eyes on a horse and for her the thrill of encountering both in a single moment was intoxicating. Pausing a moment to catch her breath, she drew back the door flap and stepping through the opening, she entered the long-house.

An aisle some six feet wide ran down the centre of the dimly lit building, with rows of compartments of a similar size on both sides. Each was separated from the other by a screen or partition fashioned from boards made from bark held in place by upright stakes. Ducking into one of the room, Minawa reached for a bundle of furs and threading her fingers through the strip of rope that held them together she tried to lift it. Instantly a sharp pain knifed through her stomach and dropping the bundle she pressed both hands across her navel and clamped her teeth together to suppress the cry that threatened to burst from her mouth.

An instant later and Shingas appeared behind her, his eyes blazing with anger. Startled, she looked up at him and instantly regretted her foolishness. Admonished she lowered her gaze and without a word Shingas reached down, lifted up the heavy bundle of furs and with Minawa in his wake, he strode out of the building.

When the pair reached the quadrangle it was already a hotchpotch of activity, with people coming and going, their strident voices adding to the general hubbub. Cooking-fires, tended by wizened old grandmothers with limbs like wire, dotted the open ground. At two of them, a large kettle filled with corn-porridge, warmed its bottom in the flames. At others, meat burned or went uncooked depending which side faced the fire, its minders too busy with women's chatter to give much thought to turning it.

Children, free from restraint ran about playing their games, their screeches accompanied by howls from the pack of camp-dogs adding to the clamorous din. Two of the older boys, emboldened by curiosity, wove their way through the legs of the warriors gathered around the whiskey barrels and holding out their hands with palms cupped, they begged a drop of the liquid. Linnet saw them first and amused by their impudence, was about to give them a taste when Flute grabbed his arm and cursing him for his intended stupidity, swung his foot at the two scallywags and sent them scampering away.

Now scores of poker-faced warriors, their cache of pelts carried in their arms or in loose bundles over their shoulders, made their arrival and congregating about the traders, with discerning eyes they examined the trade goods displayed on the ground to tempt them. Close on the heels of these successful hunters were their squaw's; round-faced maidens got up in all their finery, their hair shiny with bear grease, their high cheeks powdered with vermilion and each of them hopeful of some new adornment. Shingas and Minawa mingled among them, her eyes bright with anticipation as she viewed the assortment of trinkets and baubles, each as alluring to her as the trays of diamonds and rubies displayed in a jeweller's shop window would be to a genteel lady.

Away from the melee a large crowd of warriors had gathered around the whiskey barrels, all eager to exchange an exquisite fur for a swallow of the fiery liquid. Several of the older squaws looked on with trepidation and knowing from experience the bouts of madness the evil water would inflict on their menfolk, several quickly slipped away to their rooms and put his knife and tomahawk away from sight. Even among those warriors clamouring for a cupful, there were some who knew full well its effects but still drank with disregard.

But hunger was also a magnet and as the aroma of hominy and roasting meat filled the breeze-less air, people gathered around the fires eager to satisfy their appetites. Soule, confident if only for a short time, to leave others to manage the business of trade, had already been lured to one of the bonfires and now helped himself to a cut of tasty meat. Seated at his feet with their fat bottoms in the dirt, just feet from the low flames in which the skinned carcasses of two dogs slowly roasted, were two naked infants each chewing with relish on a titbit given to them by their mother. But what took Soule's attention and held his gaze were the four warriors standing in a tight group beside one of the buildings. All of their savage faces were emblazoned with war-paint and they were armed with knives and hatchets. Detached from the activity all around them and at times made invisible to him by the clamour and confusion of the moment, when he was permitted a good sight of them he saw upon each dark face the shadow of conspiracy. A moment later and they were lost to him completely when a squaw threw a stick into the fire and a myriad of sparks flew up into the air and blotted out his view. When the chance came to see them again, they were gone, disappearing as though they had been an apparition. But he knew they had been real and their bold, dark expressions had conveyed a warning. As he moved away from the fire and made his way back to his place at the 'counter' he promised himself to keep a watch out for them.

As Soule had watched, others were also watching. Perched high up on the outstretched branch of a withered oak a pair of ravens, the bright sunlight reflecting off their glossy wings, looked down with beady black eyes on the activity below them. The two birds often used this perch, the branch below, stained by their droppings, a chronicle to their numerous visits. They were not alarmed by the noise and commotion and today the ones who shot up at them with hard tipped arrows, were too busy with other things to bother them. Although prompted by curiosity, the real reason for their visit was seeing the women going about the camp catching and killing young dogs for the fire. Hunger was also a reason for them to watch and wait..

As the whines of the luckless ones carried up to them, they watched an old woman drinking the hot blood that spilled into her cupped hands from a dog's opened throat. Watched as the skinning knives did their work and the camp dogs impaled on spits were set over the fire to roast in its flames. Beyond where the picketed horses stood pestered by clouds of flies, they also saw groups of young girls returning from the woods carrying baskets filled with berries and wild fruit. They saw too a boy, no more than five, snatch up his puppy and with it clutched to his chest, scamper away through the maze of long-houses and disappear into the forest beyond.

But what interested them most were the pile of diaphanous entrails, entwined like a writhing mass of mating vipers, lying discarded beside the roasting fires with only the moment of opportunity separating these choice bits from their beaks. When their chance came they swooped down with the boldness of eagles, snatching up their glistening prizes and with a caw of triumph, they carried them off into the dark recesses of the forest to feast on at their leisure.

Away from the cooking fires, one of Kiashuta's warriors, the livid patch of burned flesh marking him out, pushed his way through the jostling crowd surrounding the trio of whiskey barrels. Flute and Linnet were doing good business, the growing pile of pelts at their feet a testament to their success.

Nearing the inner ring of the encircling crowd the scar-faced warrior unsheathed his knife and held it hidden down at his side. All around him Seneca warriors clamoured to be served, each clutching a gourd or other such vessel in one hand and a fur in the other. Once served they gulped down the fire-water in ravenous swallows and clamoured for more. Swaying about on unsteady legs and adding to the general confusion were the early drinkers, who having already downed several cups, were quickly succumbing to the sensations of drunkenness.

With sleeves rolled up, Linnet dipped his tin cup into the barrel of raw whiskey and smiling brightly, he turned to serve his next customer. Two warriors faced him, pushing and shoving, each determined to have his cupful first, their angry voices rising above the din. In the confusion the scar-faced warrior seized his moment and stepping forward, with a violent upwards thrust, he plunged the blade of his knife deep into the lanky youth's heart.

With a look of agony on his face Linnet staggered back clutching his chest, blood gushing from the deep wound. Screaming out, his legs buckled under him and unable to stand, he fell backwards against the barrel and sprawled full length onto the ground. For a moment his body jerked and twisted in a violent convulsion and then he lay still. Beside him whiskey spilled from the overturned barrel and washed around his lifeless body before soaking away into the dry earth.

With the deed done, the scar-faced warrior stepped back into the throng of warriors and unnoticed slipped away into the crowd, the knife held at his side, its once gleaming blade now dripping with Linnet's blood.

Soule raced across the quadrangle, pushing aside anyone in his path, the hubbub subsiding in his wake. Reaching the barrels, he saw Flute standing quite alone, the crowd of warriors kept back as though by a ring of fire. One of the barrels had been overturned and stretched out beside it was Linnet. His hands were clutched to his crimson chest like talons, a dam-in-vain against the spill of blood from the deep wound beneath them which ran in rills along his bare arms and pooled on the dry ground. Dropping onto his knees beside him, Soule ran his fingers across Linnet's eyes, closing them shut.

Like a trapped animal' Flute cast fearful glances at the encircling ring of Indians then dropping down onto one knee he pressed his lips to Soule's ear. When he spoke, his breath stank of whiskey.

'There was a shouting-row, I didn't see it started but when I turned to look, I seen this painted heathen with his knife pushed into poor Linnets chest and him screaming like a pig. Was nothing I could do Quinty, I knew he was done for, none screams that way and lives.'

The man's words washed over Soule, he himself knew more of what had happened than Flute, even though he hadn't witnessed the act. But he couldn't confess to it. He couldn't even ask Flute to point out the culprit for he knew that the one who had murdered Linnet would have made his escape by now, his bloody knife clutched in his hand like a trophy.

Slowly, Soule climbed to his feet. When he spoke it was with a heavy heart.

'Stay with him.'

And with that he turned to walk away, his mind alert to the possibility that unless he dealt with matters in a resolute fashion, then they may all suffer Linnet's fate.

Before he could take two paces, Bailey, Doublejohn and McCallum, each clutching their musket, broke through the crowd of onlookers and closed around him. Grim faced, with hammers cocked, they stared at the multitude of people milling around them, expecting at any moment to hear the shriek of the war-cry and have every warrior in the crowd fall on them with their knife and tomahawk raised.

'Steady lads.' Even as Soule spoke, as if by magic a section of the encircling crowd parted to form a broad avenue and flanked by a dozen armed warriors Wapontak strode purposefully towards the group of fur-traders. At his shoulder, with a war-club resting lightly in the hollow of his arm was Pahotan. Stopping a pace of two in front of Soule, the old Sachem looked beyond him towards the barrels and the prostrate body of Linnet. More in pantomime than purpose, Soule half turned and pointed an accusing finger at the corpse.

'Do you see, one of my men is killed? Murdered by one of your warriors.' Soule's voice rang with anger. 'Are we all to be killed? Is this your bloody plan?'

Wapontak listened calmly to the man's vehement outburst, his own emotions concealed behind an impenetrable veil. He knew this was the work of Kiashuta, that his black heart had conjured up this deed in the hope of en-flaming the tribe's young warriors into an orgy of killing. Turning his head towards Pahotan he spoke a few words in a hushed tones and immediately Pahotan gestured to a group of warriors and together they jogged away towards where a narrow path led into the forest and in a moment all were swallowed up by the dark curtain of spruce.

Turning his gaze on Soule, Wapontak placed his right hand over his heart, the gesture signifying that the words he spoke were truthful.

'No one among my people has committed this evil thing. There have been others here, bad Indians who would have us take up the hatchet against the English. I have sent my warriors to find the ones who did this so that they may be brought back to answer for their crime.'

Soule knew the old Sachem spoke the truth, the real blame he knew rested with him. He had known with certainty that the ones he had seen were troublemakers sent to stir up unrest and that he should have kept a better eye on them. He thought of the bloody trophy the five now had to show and cursed his carelessness. Before he could respond, a disturbance in the crowd distracted him and turning to see its cause, he saw Blessing bullying his way through the crowd. Instantly Soule moved towards him, hoping to reach him before he saw Linnet's body but he was too late.

When he caught sight of Linnet's corpse sprawled out on the ground Blessing let out a low moan and for a moment it seemed he would run towards it. But instead he turned his head away and fixing his small piggy eyes on Wapontak he let out an agonising cry and lumbered towards him, his right hand striving to free the hatchet stuck in his belt. More accustomed to the man's usual ponderous manner, his speed of action took Soule by surprise. Recovering, he rushed forward and met Blessing's charge with his own, his shoulder hitting hard into the man's bear-like chest, his left hand gripping Blessing's wrist and preventing him from freeing his hatchet.

'Hold back you fool, would you have us all killed?'

His plea fell on deaf ears and straining to free his axe Blessing surged forward, rage fuelling his strength but as he did so a sharp pain in his side caused him to stop. Puzzled by the sensation he stepped back and with his free hand he touched his fingers to the fleshy spot just below his last rib. Taking them away, he peered down and saw that they were covered in blood and he knew instantly he had been stabbed.

'I'll kill you fore I let you past. You knows I mean it.'

There was venom in Soule's voice but what concerned Blessing more was the certainty that he would do it. Although the wound in his side was not a deep one, it was enough to deflate his anger and so freeing his wrist from Soule's grip, he turned and with ponderous steps made his way towards Linnet's body. The lad had been his good and dear friend, in truth he had been more, though few knew it. For now though he was forced to swallow the bitterness of his frustrated rage, but he knew that if he were patient that the moment for retribution would present itself and Linnet's murder would be revenged.

Bending down, Blessing slipped his powerful arms under Linnet's body and with seemingly effortless ease, lifted him up. Standing for a moment he looked down at the youth's pox scarred face. The mask of pain which, moments before had distorted it was replaced now by a look of calm repose. On steady legs, with only eyes following him, Blessing walked slowly towards the encircling forest, his bearing as dignified as any undertaker.

In his wake, with the distraction over, festivities began again and warriors and squaws drifted back to the cooking-fires and the dwindling piles of trade goods still to be haggled over. Noise rose up and robbed the silence, children returned to their boisterous games, squaws chattered like fishwives around the fires and warriors pressed once more around the two remaining barrels, clamouring for a cup of the liquid, which burned their throats and addled their brains.

With mixed emotions, Soule stood and watched Blessing disappear into the gloomy woods. As well as a feeling of sadness at the lad's untimely death, he was also angry with himself for his failure in trying to preventing it. His only consolation, small though it was, was in knowing that for all his young years, Linnet had been aware of the dangers men like themselves faced and knew that sometimes death was the price exacted on them. His thoughts were broken by the appearance of Pahotan and his warriors as they emerged in single file from the forest.

The very fact that they were alone told him all he needed to know. The murderers were gone, the chance to punish the guilty one was lost.

Once clear of the village, the young boy with the puppy still clutched in his arms crossed a wide ditch grown over with grass and plunged into the forest, a place of trees and hiding places. After minutes of running he stopped in front of an ancient hemlock. The tree had died long ago but could not lay down to decay, being snarled in the strong branches of a neighbour. Its own branches had rotted and crumbled away and were now no more than a random trellis for vines and creepers to exploit. Above, sunlight peeped in through the torn canopy and touched yellowing fingers upon its decayed length, while born in the black mould exposed by its half drawn roots, fern and wild flowers prospered. On hands and knees, his puppy held tightly under a skinny arm, the boy pushed and crawled a way through the trespassing foliage until he reached the bower beneath the great tree, a room of stem and leaf, damp and dark but a fine hiding place for a small boy.

And so he sat with the puppy licking his face, outside the world was silent and they were invisible to it, even small noises were lost in the puppys' tongue. The boy had a pouch suspended on a cord around his neck, an old tobacco-pouch which, had belonged to his grandfather and every now and then he would reach in and remove a small morsel of meat and feed it to the pup.

They stayed and were silent and still for what was for ones so young, a long time. But now the puppy struggled even harder to be let free and so the boy crawled out from the hiding place and walked away but not towards the village, it was too early to go home for there might yet be those who were still hungry.

The boy had almost reached the small clearing where they would be safe to play, when he suddenly stopped in his tracks. Ahead of him straddling the narrow trail like a colossus was Blessing, with Linnet's lifeless body cradled in his arms. It was as though they had suddenly risen up from the ground. The boy's first instinct was to flee but then he saw that he knew them, remembered that he had run beside them that morning as they entered the village and so recognition with a little help from curiosity, put paid to caution and when Blessing laid Linnet's body onto the ground and beckoned him forward saying.

'Come up boy, come close and see a dead man, Tody here won't mind you staring.'

Although he had no understanding of the words the man spoke, the gesture was plain enough and innocent of all thoughts of danger he walked up and stood looking down on Linnet's prostrate body. The puppy's instincts were stronger and he wriggled frantically to be free.

Suddenness as always gave little warning and now there was no time to even cry out as Blessing's powerful hands closed like a chocking collar around his thin neck. The puppy was dropped and ran away into the trees as the boy consumed by fear and terror struggled frantically to free himself. But the beating of his small fists against Blessing's chest were as futile as a butterflys' wings on a pane of glass and with a simple twist of his wrists Blessing snapped the boy's neck like a dry twig.

Dropping the lifeless child onto the ground, Blessing stooped and lifting up Linnet's body he walked away. But after taking only a few paces he stopped, turned around and looked back at the body of the child. With his mind made up, Blessing walked back to the boy and setting down his burden, he pushed aside the foliage beside the trail and peered into the darkness beneath the skirts of the spruce trees. He would bury the pair here, it was a good enough spot and would save him more carrying.

So Blessing became a burrowing animal, tearing at the soft mould and beneath it the rich soil with his axe and clawing fingers. It was hard and sweating work but he worked tirelessly. The wound in his side began to bleed again but he paid it no heed. Long minutes passed and at last it was done and Blessing sank back against the heaped earth and filled his lungs. But his rest was short and he began again with the burial. Linnet was first to be put into the grave, then the child was laid face uppermost upon his bloody chest. They fitted snug in the measured hole. Dropping to his knees Blessing lowered his head and with uncharacteristic gentleness, he kissed Linnet upon the lips, then without prayer or farewell words, began filling in the hole, heaping the earth into the familiar mound above it and firming it with his hands. With a finger he wrote Linnet's name into the soil, then turned and walked out from the spot.

Emerging from behind the curtain of spruce branches Blessing stood for a moment and looked around with a malevolent eye for the boy's puppy. Disappointed, he turned and with lumbering strides made his way back along the narrow trail to the Seneca village.

Already the day was ageing, the clamour of trading had ended and the moment caught its breath. Weary children rubbed their tired eyes and indolent warriors lounged about the dying fires, while those who had drunk their fill at the whiskey barrels succumbed to its effects and slept where they had fallen. Seated in doorways their hands and tongues rarely still, mothers and grandmothers took their ease, while only the occasional belligerent snarls of scavenging camp-dogs intruded upon the air of tranquillity which prevailed.

Outside the entrance of the long-house, which was to be their lodgings for the night, Bailey, McCallum and Doublejohn busied themselves sorting and tying the bounty of bartered pelts into bundles. Not a bead or blanket remained of the trade goods, even the whiskey barrels were empty, their contents sold to the last drop. With his counting done, Soule put away his tally-paper and sharpened charcoal. Although pleased with the good business they had done he was conscious of the mood of melancholy which hung over his men following Linnet's death. He saw it in the urgency with which they worked, just how eager each of them was to be gone from this place.

Moments later he was jolted out of his contemplative mood by the sound of Bailey's voice raised in anger and turning to discover its cause he saw the trader and a Seneca warrior confronting one another and Bailey's hand resting on the handle of his axe. In a dozen strides Soule was across to them and knotting his hands in Bailey's coat front he dragged him away.

'Are you gone mad?'

Although kept low his voice was imbued with vehemence. Letting his anger subside, Soule released his grip and turned to face the man's antagonist.

Shingas stood before him on lost legs, swaying yet never quite losing his balance. His eyes were shot with drunkenness, his savage features stripped of their menace and held in his outstretched hand was the beautiful fur of a winter fox.

'Whisky.' Although the word was slurred, Soule understood the warrior's request.

'There is no whiskey. Whiskey is gone.'

He spoke in a firm voice, his tone emphatic. Perplexed, Shingas shook his head slowly from side to side and holding out his arm, he pointed to where the three whiskey barrels stood and said again.

'Whiskey!'

Without replying, Soule turned on his heels and pulling his axe from his belt, he crossed to the barrels, tipped one over onto its side and with a powerful downward strike he staved it in.

'Whiskey is gone! No whiskey!'

Hopeful that the demonstration had convinced Shingas that the barrels were dry, Soule strode across to Bailey and pulling the man's axe from his belt he turned to Shingas, snatched the proffered fur from his grasp and thrust the axe into his hand. Shingas focussed his blurring gaze on the axe. He was pleased with his new hatchet, it felt good in his hand. Seeing his trade accepted, Soule turned to the others and said 'Come lads, tis time to fill our empty bellies.'

And with that he led them into the long-house where as a gesture of hospitality a meal had been prepared for them.

Squatting around the low fire, with great relish they tucked into the food warming over the charcoal embers, each of them as rapturous over the flesh of dogs basted in sunflower oil as an English squire over his dish of oven roasted partridge marinated in red wine and drizzled with wild honey.

Shingas staggered away, the feeling of pleasure at his trade quickly lost in the mood of depression which consumed him. Like others of their race, the Seneca found no happiness in their drinking, maudlin sorrow or violent rage were the only rewards for their indulgence. With the strength in his legs growing weaker, only will power kept him from falling to the ground, that and the tinkling bell of consequence warning him that he must find his couch before this sickness consumed more of his faculties.

With his long-house in sight, Shingas was stopped on his stumbling journey by seeing Minawa, a new red blanket draped over her shoulders, standing with a group of young squaws. Strutting about before these radiant maidens were youthful dandies, done up in their foppery of plumes and beads, their lithe bodies anointed with scented oil, basking in the flirtatious glances of the young squaws.

Eagerly, Shingas' invidious mind revealed itself, showing him not the naturalness of the scene, its harmless nature but only that these young men were paying his squaw compliments with their eyes. Aroused, jealousy welled up in him and enraged he became its plaything.

Screaming out in anger Shingas ran towards the half dozen or so young men, their faces turned towards him in disbelief. In a moment he was among them, striking out with his axe. Consumed with fear the young maidens fled in all directions like frightened chickens chased by a fox. Youthful gallants without the ties of warrior-hood also turned and ran as he swung his axe at them in wild arcs. One youth, pride overcoming fear, stood his ground and he became the anvil for Shingas' rage.

Horrified, Minawa rushed up to him, reaching out she gripped his upraised arm in her hands and pleaded with him to stop. Shingas looked at her with eyes that didn't know her and reaching out with his free arm he struck her hard across the face and sent her reeling backwards onto the ground. Slowly, Minawa climbed onto her feet and flinging herself forward she clung to his legs, her voice, her whole being imploring him to stop. Blind with rage, Shingas raised the axe in the air and striking downwards with terrible force, he sank its steel head into her skull. Instantly blood gushed from the terrible wound and Minawa's lifeless arms slipped from around his legs and she slumped backwards onto the ground like a discarded doll.

Immediately the bloody act freed the youth of his pride and turning his back on the horror he had witnessed, he fled towards the safety of the encircling long-houses. With a savage cry Shingas gave chase but in moments his false strength ebbed away and after a short stumbling run, his unsteady legs gave way and he fell against the wall of a long-house, his head striking the corner post and plunging him into unconsciousness.

Later when the village slept, cloaked in darkness, Pahotan and another warriors came to where Shingas lay and lifting him up in their arms, they carried him into his room and laid him on his couch. Waiting until the young warrior had slipped away through the open doorway, Pahotan pulled a blanket around his shoulders and seated himself cross-legged on the ground.

Shingas woke slowly, his forehead throbbing, his throat dry and raw. Lifting his hand, he laid a finger on the bruised and swollen lump just above his left eye, the epicentre of the pain which lanced through his head with the regularity of a heartbeat. Perplexed, he distracted himself by reaching for the earthenware pitcher beside his couch and pressing it to his parched lips he drank greedily from it, gulping the water down in great swallows, thankful for its coolness on the scalded flesh of his throat. Only when his thirst was quenched and he had set the pitcher onto the ground did he notice the figure seated on the rush mat floor opposite him. But before he could speak, Pahotan reached out his arm and without a word, he laid Baileys blood-stained axe at Shingas' feet.

Shingas stared down at the bloodied hatchet and instantly sadness and remorse enveloped him. But their pain was not allowed onto his face, even in the shadowy darkness of his room he would not let these emotions manifest themselves. Now anger snapped at their heels and they were gone. As always, anger must be a warrior's sadness, true born, no apparition of the whiskey barrel. For an instant its rage blighted his face, then ran like quicksilver into his coal black eyes. His anger was for the guilty, the blame belonged to these English dogs, in his invidious mind he was blameless, these Yenge had poisoned him with their whiskey and because of it he had lost everything. And so anger quickly transmuted into a burning desire for vengeance and Shingas' life was scarred by it. Climbing unsteadily to his feet, without a word Shingas took up his musket and powder-horn and slipping his carry-all, a type of satchel with a broad strap, across his shoulder, he stepped over the bloody axe, and pulling aside the curtain he slipped out through the doorway.

Enveloped by darkness Shingas moved through the village, his only thought was to be out from this place and to find sanctuary in the solitude of the woods. Passing by one of the long-houses he checked his stride and then as if drawn by an unseen force, he moved closer to its curtained doorway. From inside the sound of women's voices singing in low tones carried to him, their song a mournful elegy. Instinctively he reached out a hand to pull aside the curtain but then instantly drew it back. He knew that inside, illuminated by tallow-candles and dressed for her burial, Minawa would be laid out on a low cot, the blood washed from her face, her hair combed to hide the terrible wound in her head. Knowing this he could not look or go inside and so Shingas turned and strode away. Nothing must be allowed to increase his sadness, his thoughts must only be of vengeance, he must carry them like a heavy stone in his heart, a terrible vengeance for Minawa had been with child and now both were gone.

Following a narrow path, Shingas moved through the forest, familiarity guiding his steps. All around him ethereal specks of moonlight danced among the towering hemlocks and away in the deeper woods the yelping of a vixen calling to her mate was the only sound to intrude upon the silence. Dawn found him at the edge of a gloomy cedar swamp, the quaggy ground covered by the prostrate trunks of decaying trees with clumps of sweet-gale scattered amongst them, their bright orange catkins sparkling like jewels in the occasional splash of sunshine. Skirting its edges, Shingas followed the narrow trail as it climbed away before him until at the foot of a steep wooded ridge he was confronted by a huge granite rock. A recumbent boulder in the shape of a coiled serpent, its scaly surface overgrown with lichens and trickling with rivulets of water which drained from the hillside above.

Approaching the boulder, Shingas took a tobacco-pouch, decorated with coloured beads, from his carry-all and laid it upon the weathered granite. Re-tracing his steps to where a rocky outcrop afforded him some concealment, he seated himself cross-legged upon the hard ground. Here and there other gifts had been placed on the craggy surface of the giant rock, pushed into crevasses or laid upon a narrow ledge; a child's moccasin, an earthen-wear pot filled with honey, each one an offering to a deity, for this was a sacred place, a holy place, a natural cathedral to the people of the Iroquois.

All that day and into the early evening Shingas sat before the great stone, stiff backed, his musket across his knees, his unwavering gaze upon its rocky surface. The gift of tobacco was for Areskoui, the God of war, it was his help that he invoked with chants and prayer but no dream or vision visited him, Areskoui's face was turned away. Fearing that the fur-traders could have left the village and would soon be beyond his vengeance, Shingas abandoned his fruitless vigil and consumed with malignity and frustration he set off homewards through the darkening forest. His life was pictured with gloom, his standing and reputation as a warrior were lost, none would snatch up the tomahawk after hearing his cry for vengeance. But his inordinate pride denied these adversities, he was a warrior of the Onundawaga, his was not a hollow name and vengeance was now his life's ruling passion and he would brave even death to sate its craving. So preoccupied was he with these thoughts, that it seemed the small sound would escape him. But then it came again, the whimpering of a young animal, the whimpering of a dog.

Even in the darkness beneath the spruce branches, Shingas' eyes found the puppy, it had unearthed one of the boy's small hands and this forbidding marker guided him to the grave. Dropping onto his knees he clawed away the mounded earth and discovered its terrible secret. Reaching down, Shingas lifted the boy out from the shallow pit and cradled him in his arms. With uncharacteristic tenderness he brushed away the dirt which still clung to his innocent face and then gently, as though fearful of waking him, he laid him on the ground. Looking down at the small lifeless figure Shingas saw in the stillness of the child's heart an omen. This foul murder would not go unpunished, unavenged, no ears would be closed to the cry for retribution and he Shingas would use the moment for his own revenge. With the thought thrilling inside his savage breast, he caught up the puppy by the scruff of its neck and pushing aside the overhanging branches, he came out from the leafy bower and with swift strides, set out along the narrow trail leading to the village.

Bathed in bright moonlight, Pahotan walked slowly between the rows of long-houses, carried in his arms was the lifeless body of the young boy. An hour earlier, Shingas had slipped into the village like an enemy and sought him out and after telling his old ally of what he had found, he had lead him and two other trusted warriors to the macabre grave. Once gathered around the gruesome spot, Pahotan told Shingas of the great concern over the missing child and how all that day bands of warriors had searched the forest for sign of him, while medicine men, beating on their magic drums and chanting mystical incantations, had called upon the great Manitou for his help. Speculation he said had been rife, some said the child had been carried off by an evil spirit in the guise of a wild beast. Others that a Huron or Ottawa war-party in search of scalps, fearful of attacking the village, had snatched the boy when he ventured into the forest. None he concluded, had suspected this terrible thing.

Now as if by magic warriors and squaws appeared and crowded around him, their discordant cries growing louder. Flaming torches lit the scene with their lurid glow and the strident wailing of the women provoked terrible howls from the camp-dogs. Suddenly a toothless old woman with sunken cheeks forced her way through the throng, jabbering and gesturing. Following in her wake was a young squaw her face lined with anguish. Reaching Pahotan's side, with a soulful cry the young mother tore her child from him and crushing his frail body to her chest, in a sobbing voice she spoke his name. But then realisation swept over her, her child was dead and with an agonising scream she sank to her knees, her tears wetting his marble face. Gentle hands led her away, other hearts sought to share her grief.

Sounds began again, angry voices were raised, questions shouted out. Where had Pahotan found the child? How had he died? Tell us! Tell us! Pahotan raised his arms and an expectant hush descended over the crowd. Waiting beyond the ring of people, the two young warriors stood like actors in the wings of a stage, each holding onto one of Linnet's legs. With a cry Pahotan called out to them, bringing them into the tragedy and immediately they walked towards him dragging Linnet's rigored body behind them like some gruesome plough. In minutes it was done, incited beyond restraint by Pahotan's words with fearful shouts the multitude, men and women and even some older children swarmed around Linnet's corpse, hacking at it with knives, sticks and tomahawks in a wild frenzy. At Pahotan's bidding, others fetched armfuls of wood and heaped it into a pyre. Touching it into life with their flaming torches, the virulent mob threw the trader's mutilated corpse into the flames and shrieking like demons they leapt about the fire in an ecstasy of loathing. With the firelight playing on his face, Shingas watched from the shadows, his eyes drinking in the orgy of hatred and seeing his hopes for vengeance becoming a reality. Satisfied with his work, Pahotan slipped away across the quadrangle and reaching the council-house he pulled aside the heavy curtain covering the entrance and stepped inside.

Seated on the low bench in the centre of the building was Wapontak, head down, his eyes staring into the embers of the dying fire at his feet. The old sachem was not alone, many of the tribe's old men, summoned by the day's events, sat close by, their blankets wrapped around them against the chill night air. A squaw appeared from a corner of the gloomy building and fed a bundle of sticks into the fire and in moments small tongues of flame licked hungrily at the fuel and a pool of light spread quickly outwards and upwards, bathing the assembly in its flickering glow. Touching a taper to one of the flames, Wapontak held it to the bowl of his pipe and drew a mouthful of tobacco smoke into his lungs. Satisfied that the pipe was lit, with a gesture he beckoned Pahotan forward. Seating himself on the rush mat across from the old sachem Pahotan waited until the plume of smoke from Wapontak's mouth had drifted upwards into the dark void beneath the arched roof before he spoke, running his eyes over the old men as they listened attentively to his words. Pahotan spoke without magniloquence, it was enough that he lied to them, telling them not the whole but only as much of the story as he dared. He and two others he said had found the boy's body lying with that of the murdered trader. Yes it had been hidden with great cunning but Tusonderongue had found it, even the moose tremble when he was in the woods. No mention could be made of Shingas' part in all this, to bring him into it would jeopardise their vengeful plan, for he knew that the old sachem was opposed to any retribution against the English and that his crafty mind would seize upon this weakness and use it to his advantages. Patiently, Wapontak listened to Pahotan's words his small black eyes stabbing at him through the swirling pipe smoke. He was angry, angered by the senseless killing of the child, angered that he did not have the power to contain its violent consequences. One among the Yenge traders was a murderer yet all were condemned and so his mind concerned itself with precautions and when he spoke this thought was paramount.

'All the whiskey-carriers must be killed, none must escape and their bodies carefully hidden. It must be as though they had been a dream.'

Pahotan nodded solemnly, respectful of the old sachem's concern, yet when he spoke his words came from an unreasoning heart and his sagacious reply touched a chord in each of the old men and the years fell away from their eyes.

'If they fight they are too few. If they run away we are too many. All will die, it will be as if they had been a dream and when the rain has washed away the marks of their horses even the dream will be forgotten.'

With his pledge given, Pahotan stood up and left them. Stepping out into the night he quickly returned to his long-house for he knew that even now warriors would be in their wigwams painting themselves for war. The mother of the dead child belonged to the totemic clan of the wolf and by virtue of the Hodenosaunee custom of descent following the female line, so also did her child. Each clan was expected to avenge wrongs committed against it and so the camp-criers went about the village their raised voices calling those warriors of the mother's totem to the war-fire.

Shingas was already in Pahotan's long-house and from the solitude of shadows he watched the comings and goings of squaws busy with the preparations entrusted to them. Faggots were fed into a starveling fire and rush-mats set upon the ground in rows about it. Trenchers of meat and other food that could be gleaned after the gluttony of yesterday was brought and put down. When all was ready they departed. One young maiden, purposely the last to leave, paused at the doorway and turned towards Shingas a coquettish smile on her face. He was now a warrior without a wife and she hoped his eyes had looked and seen her and that he would remember. Shingas fixed her with a cold stare and in an instant she was gone, hurt by his cruel eyes yet with hope still clutched to her heart.

Now they came, warriors adorned in all their savage finery, their bold features and lithe bodies smeared with paint, red for war, black for death, their scalp-locks fluttering with feathers, tomahawks and scalping knives pushed in their belts. Every fighting man of the wolf clan came and sat at Pahotan's fire and by eating of the food prepared for them, each gave a solemn promise to follow him upon the war-path and avenge the murder of the child. Seated amongst them was Shingas, his savage features freshly painted for war. He too was a warrior of the wolf totem but he did not view this as coincidence or fate, to him this was simply a manifestation of Areskoui's will.

Feasting done, with heads held high the war-party made its way in stately procession to the quadrangle. Already a savage audience crowded its dark edges, pressing forward expectantly, hushed and hungry-eyed fearful of missing the smallest sight. Moments such as these rescued their lives from boredom and although late into the night, sleep was unthinkable, it seemed only babies dared to close their heavy eyes. A bonfire blazed at the heart of the clearing, throwing warmth and light into the watcher's faces and beside it a post as tall as a man and daubed with red paint had been driven into the ground.

Suddenly a great cry went up as the war-party, with Pahotan at its head filed into the circle. Beside him, basking in the moment, Shingas cast his eyes over the watching crowd his gaze falling on a tall long-legged young squaw, her hair adorned with brightly coloured ribbons, as she pushed her way to the front of the watching crowd. Aware of his attention, Meeataho turned her face towards him and smiled flirtatiously. For a long moment Shingas' eyes lingered on her, then averting her gaze, Meeataho turned and melted away into the crowd, her heart fluttering like a trapped bird.

With a sudden cry Pahotan leapt into the circle and with savage eloquence he harangued the attentive crowd, in words and gestures he recounted his prowess as a warrior then, armed with knife and hatchet, in a primitive pantomime he enacted his exploits, striking the post as if it were an enemy and tearing the scalp from the head of the imaginary victim. One after another the warriors of the war-party followed his example, boasting their renown and rushing up to the post, which symbolised their enemy, striking it with their tomahawks and startling the night with the shriek of the war-cry. Now in untamed spontaneity all threw themselves into the dance, leaping and circling the fire, its brightness creating grotesque giants of their shadows, its flames inspiring them. Inebriated by the emotive scene, the watching crowd surged forward into the circle and abandoned themselves in barbaric mimicry, their fearful cacophony resounding into the sepulchral darkness of the forest.

CHAPTER FIVE

I T WAS AN hour before dawn when Soule woke, he had slept badly and was glad to be awake. Laid about him, barely discernible in the false light, the remainder of the brigade lay like logs in their blankets. Without a word he moved among them rousing them with his foot. First to wake was Doublejohn, and picking up his sack of fodder he crossed to the tethered horses and began feeding each one in turn a handful of corn. With no time for a fire, breakfast was the cold remains of supper, some dry strips of meat and some mouldy oat cakes washed down with water from the nearby stream. But none complained at the Spartan meal, to a man they had caught Soule's mood of foreboding and were also eager to be on their way. Willing hands loaded the heavy bales of furs onto the horses' backs and with the last strap tightened, they moved off in single file into the trees.

All morning they trudged through the vast forest, through its stillness, its towers of bark, the narrow trail running ahead of them like a will-o-the-wisp. The going was hard and Soule set a cruel pace but it was only Doublejohn who complained and then only from concern for his beloved horses. But his protests fell on deaf ears and so eventually he gave up and the brigade pressed on in silence.

The horses heard the stream long before the men caught sight of it at the bottom of the steep hillside, a silver flash of sunlight on water, glimpsed through the crowded trees. To the relief of all, Soule called a halt beside its rushing waters, a brief rest only, for his intention was to push on and be across the Genessee River before nightfall. Doublejohn and McCallum saw to the horses, mindful that they didn't drink until their bellies were swollen. To a man, the others plunged their heads into the pure cool water and slaked their thirst. Refreshed Flute saw to his duties by dipping a grubby hand into his kitchen sack and removing the last of the mouldy journey cakes and a few dry-tack biscuits for any that would take them. Bailey, greedy as always took a handful of the cakes and stuffed them into a pocket of his coat. Blessing tested his teeth on one of the biscuits but then like Soule, resorted to soaking it in the stream before risking another bite. As they chewed on their meagre meal, all hoped that once across the river their captain would let them kill a deer.

Wiping the remains of the biscuit from his mouth with his coat sleeve, Soule took Bailey aside and after whispering a few words into the man's ear, he turned to the others and called out in a firm voice.

'Move out lads.'

With Doublejohn leading and the others spread out behind him in single file, each holding onto a lead rope, the brigade forded the shallow stream. Reaching the far bank they followed the narrow trail as it hugged the side of the gently sloping hillside before plunging into the unbroken forest of spruce and fir. As instructed, Bailey remained behind and after watching until the last of the laden horses had disappeared, he waded into the purling waters and began splashing his way upstream. Reaching a spot beneath the archway of overhanging trees where the bed of the stream deepened as it swept around the base of a rocky outcrop, Bailey slung his musket over his shoulder, and finding a purchase for his hands, he began hauling himself up the face of the rock. Pulling himself upwards, as he reached for a handhold, the branch of an overhanging tree snagged in a hole in his pocket, enlarging the tear and sending crumbs and broken pieces of cake spilling out onto the rock and cascaded down into the swirling water of the stream below. With a curse, Bailey freed his coat, and pushing aside the offending branch he pulled himself onto the top of the craggy rock. Pausing a moment to catch his breath, he moved away into the crowded trees. Moments later, finding a spot from where he had a good view of the path above the fording place, the trader unslung his musket and sat himself down on the carpet of pine needles, his back against the trunk of a tree, his legs stretched out in front of him. Once settled he dug a hand into his pocket and removed what remained of Flute's cakes. Eyeing the paltry remnants lying in the palm of his hand, he cursed the tear in his pocket for the loss of his meal.

Led by Pahotan, the war-party emerged from the long-house and in single file they walked slowly through the deserted village and away into the surrounding forest. Within minutes they entered a secluded glade, the ground shrouded in mist, a prelude to a hot day. Standing in a group at its centre were a number of squaws, each of them holding a musket and powder-horn. As the warriors approached, each of them was greeted by one of the squaws who handed them their accoutrements, receiving in return any prized ornaments and amulets they wished to leave behind. Bold as a lioness Meeataho strode up to Shingas and handed him his musket and powder-horn.

Recognising the maiden Shingas looked into her face and meeting her gaze, his features softened. Meeataho caught the look and with her heart bursting with pleasure, she turned gracefully on her heels and ran across to where the other squaws stood waiting at the heart of the clearing. Suddenly, with a loud whoop Pahotan fired his musket into the air and in slow succession the others followed his example. Then, with the sound of their musket-fire reverberated through the forest, shrieking their war-cries the warriors of the wolf clan moved away in single file and were soon lost from sight, swallowed up by the serried ranks of trees.

Silently and effortlessly, the war-party jogged through the dark labyrinth of trees. Because of the hoof prints left by the pack-horses the trail was easy to follow and although it was plain from the length of the animals' strides that the brigade had hurried, it was still early morning when they came upon the remains of the trader's night camp. Dropping onto one knee a warrior pushed his hand into the grey ashes of the dead fire, learning much from the warmth still retained in its smouldering embers. Pahotan asked a question and the warrior replied with assurance, the Yenge were close and would soon be under their knives. Satisfied, like a hound with the scent of its quarry in its nostrils, Pahotan led the war-party past the piles of dung left by the horses and away into the crowded trees.

In less than an hour they reached the place where the traders had forded the stream and the thirsty warriors pressed forward, eager to quench their thirst. Instantly Shingas extended an arm and held them back, then crouching down he examined the tracks left by the traders and their animals in the soft ground. Satisfied, he waded across to the opposite bank and stooping down carefully examined the confusion of tracks, which led away from the water's edge and into the wall of giant evergreens beyond. Pleased with his discovery Shingas forded the stream once again and told Pahotan what he had found. Six men he said had entered the stream but only five had reached the other side.

Instantly, Pahotan beckoned to Tusonderongue and Cattawa, the same two young warriors who had dragged Linnet's dead body into the village. In a few words he told them what Shingas had found and then sent them upstream to find the one who had been left behind before he had a chance to give a warning the other traders. Wading into the swiftly flowing water which barely reached half way up their thigh length leggings, the pair moved away upstream, their keen eyes scouring the far bank for anything incongruous that would betray the hiding place of the one who had been left behind.

It was Tusonderongue who saw the pieces of journey cake lying scattered on the mossy surface of the rock like flecks of dandruff on a green velvet pillow and with a gesture to Cattawa the pair left the stream and began climbing the rocky outcrop. Reaching the top, they both pulled their scalping-knives from their belts and following Bailey's clumsy footprints, they moved away into the ancient pine forest.

Concealed beneath the leafy branches of the overhanging trees, Bailey lay stretched out full length on the ground, his chin resting in his cupped hands, all his attention fixed on the distant path. In an instant Tusonderongue was on him, dropping onto his back, his legs astride Bailey's prone body like a horseback rider, his free hand forcing the fur-trader's head down into the damp mould. Unable to cry out, instinctively, Bailey reached out for his musket laying beside him but even as his hand closed around the barrel, Cattawa's foot stamped down on its wooden stock, pinning the rifle to the ground. With a whoop Tusonderongue plunged his knife between Bailey's collar-bone and neck, its honed blade slicing through muscle and gristle. A violent convulsion tore through the fur-trader's body and a gush of warm blood spurted from the rupture in his throat. Holding him down until the spasm had passed, Tusonderongue pulled out his knife and slicing its blade into Bailey's head, with a shrill cry, he peeled away his scalp. Wiping the blood from his knife-blade on Bailey's hunting-frock, Tusonderongue climbed to his feet, watching as Cattawa plundered the dead man's body. Their murderous work done, with his bloody trophy tucked in his belt, Tusonderongue turned away and leaving Bailey's corpse to the mercy of scavenging animals, the two warriors made their way back towards the stream.

Unaware of Bailey's fate, the brigade, their buckskin shirts stained with sweat, followed the fast flowing stream as it wound its way through the dark recesses of the forest. Suddenly and without warning, its racing waters plunged into a deep ravine, its steep rocky sides cutting like a scar into the wooded hillside. With the roar of the raging stream in their ears and cursing the climb which lay before them, the brigade grudgingly struggled up the steep incline and moved in single file along the narrow trail which hugged the side of the ravine. Below them, glimpsed through the mingled foliage of ash, poplar and maple their curving trunks anchored to the rocky walls of the precipice by tentacular roots, the convulsing waters raced onwards to a meeting with the Cohocton river.

Above them on a steep wooded slope concealed among the trees, their painted faces a surreal camouflage in the shadowy depths beneath the curtain of outstretched branches, the war-party watched lynx-eyed as the brigade moved slowly along the trail below. Choosing his moment, Pahotan, his face masked in vermilion and soot, cried out and the muskets of the war-party exploded in a ragged volley.

Caught in the open, the wasting hail of musket balls struck men and horses with impunity. Mortally wounded, Flute and McCallum fell to the ground. In the midst of the slaughter, Doublejohn snatched up the lead-rope of one of the horses, as whinnying in terror, with blood pouring from the bullet wounds in its body, it side-stepped towards the edge of the precipice. Desperately, Doublejohn tried to halt its progress but maddened with pain the terrified animal dragged him to the edge of the ravine and unwilling to release the rope he was dragged over the edge and together they plummet down onto the chaotic mass of rocks and boulders below.

Soule, unscathed, watched in horror as maddened with fear the remaining pack-horses were driven towards the ravine. Seizing his chance, he raced forward and catching up the lead rope of one of the animals he dragged it away. With adrenalin pumping through his veins, he unsheathed his knife and with a single stroke he cut through the horse's girth strap and pulled its pack-load from its back. Behind him, like lemmings, all but one of the remaining fear-crazed animals leap into the yawning chasm and plunged to their deaths in the raging cataract below.

Setting aside their muskets, the warriors of the war-party, pulled their tomahawks from their belt and shrieking their war-cries they raced down the slope towards the stricken traders. With blood oozing from the bullet wound in his chest, Blessing watched as four warriors moved towards him, their eyes burning with hatred. Planting his feet like a Redcoat, he raised his musket and fired, watching with satisfaction as the musket ball struck a warrior in the centre of his chest, dropping him to his knees like a pole-axed steer. All too quickly another warrior was on him. Instinctively Blessing lashed out and hit him with the butt of his musket, sending the luckless warrior staggering backwards clutching his broken jaw. Undeterred, two more warriors closed on him, they had identified him as the child's killer and meant to take him alive. Realising their intentions and well aware of the horrors that would befall him should he fall into their clutches, Blessing turned and with the last of his strength, he staggered to the edge of the ravine and with his arms outstretched like a swimmer on a diving board, he threw himself headlong into the abyss. As graceless in the air as he was on land, Blessing plunged like a sack of grain onto the rocks below, his head bursting open like a melon, his lifeless body sliding off their weathered surface into the stream and tossed about like a cork in its foaming waters, his arms and legs snapping like dry twigs, it ran the gauntlet of jagged rocks.

Seeing that all was lost, Soule grabbed a handful of the horse's mane and hauled himself up onto its back and kicking hard with his heels, not caring what direction he had chosen, he urged the terrified animal into a run.

From his vantage point among the trees Shingas watched his vengeance unfold as the warriors of the war-party moved among the dead traders tearing off their scalps. Suddenly, from the corner of his eye he spotted Soule making his dash for freedom and instinctively he threw up his musket and fired. His aim was true and lowering his musket, he watched with satisfaction as the horse's front legs buckled under it as though it had tripped on a wire and it fell head down, pitching Soule onto the hard ground.

With a cry of triumph Shingas pulled his tomahawk from his belt but just as he was about to rush forward he hesitated and looked across at Cattawa standing a dozen paces away, tomahawk in hand, watching him with envious eyes. Sensing the young warrior's lust for a scalp, Shingas pushed his tomahawk back in his belt and meeting Cattawa's gaze, he gave an assenting nod. In an instant Cattawa raced away down the slope towards the stricken fur-trader.

Dazed by the fall, Soule shook his head from side to side and pushed himself up onto all fours. Before he could climb to his feet, Cattawa was upon him and with a wild cry the young warrior struck downwards with his hatchet, its steel head slicing into Soule's upturned face with sickening force, the gush of blood transforming it into a crimson mask. Drinking in the moment with satisfaction, Shingas watched as Cattawa pulled out his knife and went to work on Soule's scalp. Moments later, his bloody work done Cattawa held Soule's matted scalp aloft and shrieked out his war-cry.

With the act of vengeance completed and the remaining bodies of the dead traders thrown into the ravine, Pahotan and the warriors of the war-party made ready to leave. Miraculously, one of the pack-horses has survived and after removing its pack of pelts, the body of the dead warrior was laid across its back. Standing apart from proceedings with four young warriors grouped about him, Shingas looked on, his gaze imperturbable. Eager to be on his way, Pahotan called out to them.

'Come it is done, we go back.'

Shingas saw the glint of anger in his eyes but his mind was made up and his reply was uncompromising.

'For you it is done but for me it is not finished. I do not go back.'

Pahotan turned his gaze on Tusonderongue and Cattawa standing at Shingas' side but he knew they would not be swayed by his words. The fresh scalp hanging from each of their belts had whetted their appetite for more and he knew they would go with Shingas. Reluctantly, Pahotan moved away and crossed to the edge of the ravine. Gazing down he saw the corpses of the fur-traders and the carcasses of their pack-horse, littering the rocks below, the eddying pools already stained red with their blood. He knew wolves would find them and tear the flesh from their bodies and that fox and wolverine would carry off their bones. Trout too would rise from their deep pools among the rocks to feast on any morsels of flesh washed down to them on the swirling current. He knew soon nothing would remain as evidence of their bloody act, already these Yenge had become a dream and soon even the dream would be forgotten.

CHAPTER SIX

SAMUEL ENDICOTE HAD chosen the spot well. Situated in the lee of a broad valley the farm stood in a meadow of wild grass, tall as a man's waist and fed by a wide meandering stream. Around it, pressing in on all sides was the forest, dark and menacing but with an abundance of timber fit for tar and lumber. There were some amongst those who had chosen to remain in Norton, who said he had been foolish, headstrong even, in venturing across the Oswego River and into the wilderness beyond with all its dangers. But Samuel had paid them no heed, the wont of a new life and not temerity had caused him to uproot his family from the relative comfort of a home in the Shires and sail across a wide expanse of ocean in a ship whose leaky timbers meant hours at the pumps just to keep her afloat. It was with an eye to the future and not a whim that had brought him to this fertile valley, that and a desire to be his own man and to forge a better life for himself and his family away from the restraints and shackles of the old world. Also a man with four sons had a duty to repay God for such a blessing, to have a thought for their lot and should the chance arise, the courage to set the bearers of his lineage on a sound and righteous course.

Standing at the heart of the farm was a single storey cabin constructed with logs, each laid out horizontally, interlocking at the corners and caulked with mud. A stone chimney set with mortar dominated the end wall, and gave the building a look of permanence. Topped by a bark roof, inside its three rooms were of a good size, the largest having two small windows and a solid door made from thick oak planks. Outside, enclosed by a tall picket fence, was a kitchen garden, its dark soil planted with pumpkins, carrots and turnips. Across from the main house and at right angles to it was a large barn constructed from planks of sawn timber. With a pair of stout doors set in its centre it made a fine store room for both timber and corn and a safe home for the dozen hens which roamed freely about the yard. Facing the barn was a smaller cabin, its log walls and roof timbers set in place but as yet without shingles, windows or a door. Dug into the ground behind it was a saw-pit with piles of tree trunks, stripped of their branches stacked beside it. Surrounding it on both sides enclosed by a split-rail fence, was an acre of cultivated ground planted with Indian corn and a further acre of pasture as grazing for a pair of Devon oxen and a milk cow.

The first year had been hard. Winter froze the ground to iron and while spring had thawed it in time for planting, the fickle English corn had refused to head. Worse yet their three hogs had died of the fever. But with the warmth of summer came new hope and the crop of Indian corn they had planted now grew up straight and tall, its golden ears promising a bountiful harvest to come. The forest too had yielded up a wealth of good timber which now lay trimmed and sawn into planks of uniform length, neatly stacked inside the barn awaiting transport to Norton, where it was sure to fetch a good price. And so it was as he sat in his high-backed chair by the evening fire, smoking his pipe, that Samuel Endicote viewed his bold endeavour with pride. He had secured a future for his sons and this rich fertile valley would be their inheritance.

Adam's welfare had long been a concern to him, but now with the prospect of his impending marriage to the woman Esther, even this burden was lifted from his shoulders. The thought that it might well be a childless union troubled him little, for with three other sons to sire him grandchildren, his lineage was assured. Besides which although she was no beauty, he had seen the desire in Saul's eyes when his gaze fell on Mistress Colwill. He had heard him on more than one occasion tiptoeing to her bed in the dead of night, so he knew with some certainty that with a husband, no matter how simple, to claim as its father, it would not be too long before she bore Saul's bastard. Morally the thought abhorred him but his conscience was appeased in knowing that at least the child would have Endicote blood in its veins. The only mystery was that it hadn't already happened.

Kit, a boy aged about ten with a sunburned face and long straw coloured hair walked out from the surrounding forest and squinting against the bright sunlight he slung his squirrel-gun over his skinny shoulder and began running helter-skelter towards the farm. Bounding along beside him, its tongue lolling from its open mouth was Pharaoh a large black and tan hunting dog. Clearing the fence in a single leap the hound waited patiently as Kit clambered up and over the stout lengths of wood and dropped down on the other side. Reunited, the pair then walked along between the ordered rows of corn towards the cabin where a wisp of black smoke rose from its chimney like a cat's tail.

As boy and hound emerged from the cornfield, Esther spotted them through the half open barn door and freeing herself from Saul's embrace she began buttoning up her bodice. Puzzled by her actions Saul looked at her quizzically.

'What's wrong?'

'Kit is coming.'

Smiling reassuringly Saul reached out for her.

'You worry too much, he'll not come in here.'

Esther pushed his hands away. 'He may do, we must be careful.'

Sensing her insistence, Saul scowled and moved away into the shadowy interior. Composing herself, Esther picked up the basket filled with eggs lying at her feet and pushing against the heavy barn door she stepped outside and fell in beside Kit as he walked past.

Surprised, Kit looked up at her and beamed, happy as always to see her. Keeping a straight face Esther said in a matter-of-fact voice.

'Your Ma has been calling for you.'

Kit looked sideways at her, hoping to see that she was teasing him.

'You've been off in them woods again haven't you?' She spoke the words more as a statement of fact than a question.

Kit dropped his head, he knew she was scolding him but he was determined to say nothing.

'You know your Pa forbids it.'

Knowing he had been found out, Kit pleaded.

'You won't tell will you Esther? Say you won't tell.'

Esther looked at his wretched face and her resolve weakened.

'I might... It all depends.'

Knowing she wouldn't Kit smiled from ear to ear, only to have it wiped away an instant later when the cabin door opened and Mrs Endicote stepped outside, her stern features locked in a frown. A tall woman with bright piercing eyes and a chest like a pouting pigeon, she wore a full-length linen frock with an apron tied about her waist. Her greying hair was pulled back behind her head and held in place by a plain ribbon. Fixing her gaze on Esther, she spat out her words without fear of being answered back.

'I declare girl I've never known anyone take so long to fetch a few eggs.' Then turning on Kit, 'and you, you young scallywag, you're never here when I needs you. Be off now and tell your brothers to come to the table.'

Thankful at being spared a tongue lashing or worse for his absence, Kit turned and ran off towards the saw-pit, the dog bounding along beside him. Wiping her hands purposefully on her apron Mrs Endicote turned on her heels and flounced back through the open doorway with Esther following a step behind her.

Barely a mile away from the isolated farm, Shingas and his small war-party, with Tusonderongue at its head, moved in single file through the gloomy forest. With a flint-lock carried loosely in their hands and a bullet-pouch slung around their necks, they clambered over the decaying carcasses of prostrate trees, and threaded their way through the dense pine thickets. At last with the ground sloping away before them they entered a stand of golden beech, the late afternoon sunlight filtering through their extending canopy. Suddenly Tusonderongue stopped and dropping down onto one knee he examined the patch of earth at his feet, his finger carefully tracing the outline of a small footprint impressed into the soft mould. Shingas and two of the young warriors crowded around him, staring down at the tell-tale mark. Cattawa wandered off a little way searching the ground with his eyes. Moments later he called out to the others, he had found Pharaoh's paw prints.

With the meal over, Esther and Mrs Endicote began clearing away the cups and plates, stacking them beside an oval tin bowl filled to the brim with scalding hot water. Scraping the table-scraps into a wooden trencher, Esther handed it to Kit, who smiled and hurried outside to feed them to his dog. Saul and his brother Joshua, a head shorter than Saul but endowed with the same good looks and dark hair as his elder sibling, sat taking their ease at the table. There was work to be done but after such a hearty meal a late start suited them both. Their moment of relaxation was cut short however when an inner door opened and Samuel Endicote strode into the room. At his shoulder was Adam, his eldest son. Resembling his father in height and build, Adam had his mother's countenance, except for the eyes, for where hers were like two bright buttons, his were pale and listless and gave his featureless face a doleful look. Like all the men of the household he wore a loose cotton shirt, buckskin leggings and a pair of sturdy leather boots.

The clock on the mantel-shelf struck the hour and Samuel looked toward his wife.

'We'd best be leaving.'

As she was accustomed to, Mrs Endicote nodded her head in agreement. Samuel turned to the two idlers lounging at the table and with more than a hint of annoyance in his voice, he spoke sharply to them. 'Bring up the wagon. Look lively now.'

Obediently, Saul and Joshua got to their feet and left the room without a word.

Clutching a laden satchel, Mrs Endicote crossed to her husband and slipped the strap over his shoulder, pecking his cheek with her dry lips as she did so.

'I've packed a slice of venison pie for you both and a little of the cake left over from supper. Doubtless Minister Rathbone will provide you with supper, so twill suffice till then.'

It was plain from her tone that there would be no more provisions even if he chose to ask. Plunging the plates and pots into the hot water, Esther busied herself with the washing-up. From the corner of her eye she caught sight of Adam hovering by the door watching her, hoping she would look up and see his smile. Disappointed, he turned away and followed his father outside.

At the edge of the forest, hidden in the shadows cast by the overhanging trees, Shingas and his war-party looked down on the farm below nestled in the valley, their sharp eyes missing nothing.

Moments passed and then without a word Shingas handed his musket to Cattawa and walked away down the wooded hillside and into the meadow of wild grass. Following the course of the stream until it reached the edge of the corn field he splashed across its pebbled bed and with the stealth of a predatory animal, moved along beside the split-rail fence towards the cluster of timber buildings.

Harnessed to the hitch-pole of the wagon the two oxen waited patiently in the heat of the day, their heads already pestered by a cloud of flies. Whip in hand, Samuel climbed up into the seat alongside Adam and took up the thick leather reigns. With a nod to his wife, he turned towards his three sons standing in a group awaiting their patriarch's impending departure with an air of indifference.

'No idleness while we're away do you hear? His voice as always imbued with authority. 'Yon cabin needs finishing before the week is out. See to it I'm not disappointed.'

Kit and Joshua shuffled their feet and as always left it to Saul to reply. Looking across at Esther standing in the doorway, Saul fixed her with his dark brooding eyes. Although her forthcoming marriage to Adam suited him well enough, strangely and for no reason that he could fathom, he now found the arrangement wholly disagreeable to him. Had he not been such a stranger to the emotion, he might more readily have recognised, that the cause of this confusion was plain jealousy.

'Aye father we'll see to it that the newly-weds have a roof over their heads before their wedding night.'

Ignoring the acrimony in Saul's reply, Samuel shouted out.

'Hey up! Hey up!' And with an encouraging crack of the whip the team of oxen strained against the yoke and slowly the wagon, heavily laden with sawn lengths of timber, lumbered forward, its four iron rimmed wheels finding and following in the deep ruts in the track, a track which would take them to the river and beyond it, to the small settlement of Norton.

Without waiting to see the wagon out of sight, the three brothers turned and ambled away towards the saw-pit. Lagging behind, Kit cast a forlorn look over his shoulder at Pharaoh, chained to his post outside the cabin, clearly remembering his mother's words that same morning as she fastened the chain to the hound's brass studded collar. 'There'll be no wandering off into yonder woods for you and your hound while your father's away. Do you hear?'

Shingas watched the wagon's departure with mounting interest, and pleased with what he was witnessing, he slipped silently back into the meadow and following the direction the wagon had taken, moved away towards the encircling forest. Once among the rigid spires of spruce and fir Shingas dropped down from the high ground and keeping the track in sight as it wound along the foot of the slope, he moved at a steady jog through the thinning trees until he reached the river.

It was an hour before the laden wagon reached the river, a nameless tributary of the Oswego, its broad eddying current flowing with a gentle murmur beneath the arching foliage of ash and maple. With a crack of the whip Samuel urged the reluctant team into the fording-place and with the waters reaching up to their bellies, the panting oxen, their tongues lolling from their jaws, hauled the heavy cart across to the far bank and on into the dark bosom of the forest beyond.

Hidden in the deep shadows beneath the towering trees, motionless as a statue, Shingas watched the cart until it disappears from sight. With night already drawing its curtain of darkness over the day and confident that the wagon would not be returning, he slipped away and following the rutted track, jogged back towards the Endicote's farm.

The small township of Norton sat on a large patch of cleared ground beside the Oswego River at a point where it narrowed between low banks and the shallow water and stony bed made it an ideal fording place. Its single street which ran parallel to the river was lined on both sides by cabins and the occasional clapper-board house, the light from their windows and porch lights illuminating its hard packed surface. A forge stood at the far edge of the town's limits, its furnace glowing with a bright orange light as the blacksmith worked on into the night. The clang of his hammer ringing out, as with sweat and craft he worked his magic on the super-heated length of metal laying before him on the horn-tipped anvil.

With a final crack of the whip Samuel urged the oxen up the sloping bank and into the street, eventually bringing the wagon to a halt in front of a wide windowless building fronted by a pair of heavy doors and set above them, just visible in the closing darkness, a white painted board with the words 'Zebadiah Clemens – Merchant' painted on it in nine inch tall black letters. No sooner had the weary beasts dropped their heads, than one of the doors swung open and Zebadiah himself, a stockily built, middle-aged man dressed in coarse linen trousers and a sky-blue smock-coat stepped outside. Holding the lantern he carried aloft, he called out in a voice infused with a broad Lincolnshire dialect 'Lord love us Samuel Endicote what hour is this to be disturbing honest folk taking their supper.'

Although his face was set in a grimace, the humour in his voice, betrayed his annoyance as a parody. Climbing down from the wagon, Samuel took hold of Zebadiah's extended right hand and gripping it tightly, he replied.

'And since when did Norton's merchants keep shopkeepers' hours?'

A contrived look of horror appeared on the merchant's open face.

'Mercy be what a terrible thought.'

No sooner had he spoken when the other door was flung open and four men, their loose fitting shirts rolled up at the sleeve and tucked into the waist of their wadmal trousers, appeared and without needing to be told, began unloading the lengths of timber from the wagon and carrying them into the dark interior of the warehouse.

'Will you and the lad join my good lady and myself at our table Samuel?'

'Thank you kindly for your offer Zebadiah but we've business to attend to with Minister Rathbone.'

'And what of food and lodgings for the night? Only I hear tell that our parson is not so generous with his deeds as he is with his words, more especially where absentee parishioners are concerned.'

Samuel stared back at him, a flicker of amusement in his eyes 'Best you leave your storehouse door open then if what you say of his lack of hospitality is true.'

'That I will. Now be off with you, my men will see to your oxen.'

'And what of my furniture. Do you have it?'

'Aye every last stick and all stored safely under my roof ready to be loaded for your return.'

With that the two men shook hands once more and with Adam following a step behind, Samuel turned and walked away down the street towards the town's church.

To call it a church only would be wrong, for the building mainly served as the town's Meeting-house, only being given over twice a week for religious business. On the Sabbath as expected and on a Thursday, when Minister Rathbone gave an evening sermon for those pious souls in the community who needed to receive the word of God more frequently than on the church's allotted day. Dominating the building's frontage was an imposing doorway with a casement window set on either side like a pair of all-seeing eyes. While the building itself stood in darkness the clapper-board house alongside it, so close as to be almost joined to it, showed a light at one of its downstairs windows, a beacon to which Samuel strode towards. Upon reaching the entrance, he lifted the brass door-knocker and brought it down with a resounding bang.

Almost immediately the heavy door was opened by a young girl carrying a lantern. She was simply dressed in a smock-frock of coarse white linen, with a lace edged coif framing her pallid face. Samuel stared at her for a moment, thinking she might speak first. Disappointed, he stepped closer into the light.

'Good evening Missy my name is Endicote, I'm here to see Minister Rathbone.'

With a fleeting smile the young girl ushered them inside.

'You're expected sir. Kindly follow me if you will and I'll take you to him.'

Retracing her steps, the maid led them along the narrow hallway. Tapping gently on a door, she turned the handle and pushed it open.

'If you please sir, Mr Endicote and his son are here.'

Stepping past her, Samuel and Adam entered the large candle-lit room. Square in shape, the minister's study had a homely interior enriched somewhat by the decorative panels set into its white-washed walls, and the finely woven square of scarlet carpet which covered most of the highly polished floorboards. Standing with his back to the red-brick fireplace, was Minister Rathbone, the smoke from his long-stemmed Meerschaum pipe drifting upwards and forming a blueish haze above his balding head. Although the same age as Samuel, his portly figure and soft hands showed him to be a man wholly unaccustomed to manual work of any kind. He wore a long black frock coat with deep velvet cuffs, a coat more fitting for a bishop than a parson. Under it and of equal quality, was a shirt of sheer-spun white linen with a plain wide collar. Hanging from a chain about his ample neck, was a cross of solid gold. Setting his pipe down on the mantel, he extended his arms in a practised gesture and in a deep sonorous voice greeted his guests.

'Welcome Samuel. Welcome.' Then turning to the young maid, 'you may fetch supper my child, I am certain our guests are sorely in need of sustenance.'

Minister Rathbone watched her depart then gestured towards a pair of straight backed chairs.

'Come seat yourselves, you must be weary after your journey.'

Obediently, Samuel and Adam crossed the room and sat down on the chairs, while Minister Rathbone returned to his place in front of the fire, warming his hands behind his back.

'So Samuel and how is life in the wilderness?'

'Hard. But we are faring well. There's good timber and water and the soil is fertile.'

'And thankfully the good Lord has kept you safe from the heathen savages.'

Smarting at the Minister's sanctimonious remark, having himself more faith in a loaded musket, Samuel bit his tongue and composed a more suitable reply.

'Aye, we are safe in God's hands.'

Minister Rathbone responded to his words with a benevolent smile, then turned his gaze upon Adam.

'So Adam, you wish to be wed. I trust....'

But before he can finish the sentence Adam blurts out, his voice bursting with excitement.

'Pa is building us a cabin. Just for Esther and me to live in.'

A frown touched Minister Rathbone's face.

'Good! Yes very good but...'

Leaning forward Samuel nudged Adam with his elbow. 'Say what I have taught you' said the nudge. Slowly, Adam got to his feet, his face a picture of concentration.

'I shall be a good and dutiful husband. I... I shall take care of my new wife and see to it that no harm shall come to her. I will... I will provide for her and not be neglectful of her needs.'

'Quite so my son. Quite so.'

Before he can say more, the door opened and the young girl entered the room carrying a laden tray. Grateful for the distraction Minister Rathbone announced in a pleased tone.

'Ah supper!'

Crossing the room, the young girl put down the heavily laden tray and proceeded to set out its contents, three pewter plates, a board containing a round of cheese, a plate filled with cold cuts of meat, a bowl of pickled eggs and a basket of bread warm from the oven, onto the table. Watching her every movement like a stalking cat, Minister Rathbone's licentious gaze never left her for an instant. Conscious of his attention, with the table laid, she turned and quickly left the room.

The three men had barely taken their places at the table when she was back, this time balanced on her tray were two leathern jacks full to the brim with cider and a silver cup filled with malmsey. The jacks she placed beside Samuel and Adam, the silver cup she set down beside her employer's plate. The tracery of fine purple veins on his pallid skin evidence of the Minister's liking for the strong, sweet wine.

'Thank you my child. You may be off to your bed now. You can clear away the table in the morning.'

With a bobbing curtsey the young girl turned and hurried across the room, the wooden heels of her shoes click-clacking on the hard floor as she skirted the edges of the rich carpet and disappeared through the door.

An hour later, with the meal concluded and Adam sent to his bed, Samuel and Minister Rathbone sat opposite each other, their features bathed in the lurid glow from the guttering candles. A half empty glass decanter of ruby port stood on the table between them.

'And you are quite certain that Mistress Colwill is equally disposed to this... this arrangement?'

Samuel put his glass to his lips and drained its contents in a single swallow.

'Assuredly. Why should she not be?'

'Come now Samuel, freedom from servitude is a poor substitute for spiritual love.'

Recognising the condescension in the Minister's tone, Samuel set the glass down hard onto the table.

'She thinks it worth it. Besides, Adam loves her well enough and she is fond of the lad despite his affliction.' Then striking the table with his clenched fist, 'she has agreed. She is for the marriage.'

Wearying of the conversation Minister Rathbone leaned forward in his chair, his eyes as bright as a bear.

'Very well. As you say it appears the arrangement has merit for both parties.' Then holding out a hand, 'have you brought her indenture with you as I requested?'

Samuel, his face flushed from the port, pulled a folded paper from the pocket of his jerkin and passed it to him.

'And my fee?'

Reaching a hand into his other pocket, Samuel took out a leather pouch and dropped it onto the table, the clink of coins was unmistakable. Unfolding the document, Minister Rathbone cast his eyes over it, familiarising himself with its contents. Satisfied, he held a corner of the paper over a lighted candle and when it caught alight he threw the document into the hearth, watching with a sense of pleasure as the fire devoured it and in doing so brought salvation from servitude to a child of God.

At first light and with the chill of night still in the air, Shingas and the four Seneca warriors, their savage faces daubed with fresh war-paint, emerged from the dark wall of trees and descended as silent as shadows into the meadow. In single file they moved through the sea of damp grass, their feet and legs shrouded in the mist rising up from the stream. Splashing across to the far bank, Shingas stopped and pointed towards the smaller of the cabins silhouetted against the lightening sky, its roof resembling the skeletal remains of the upturned keel of a long abandoned ship. Without a word Tusonderongue and two warriors slipped away and following the line of the fence, they moved away towards the half completed cabin. When the three warriors had disappeared from sight, slinging their muskets across their shoulder Shingas and Cattawa climbed the split-rail fence and crept stealthily into the cornfield.

As they moved along between the rows of ripening corn, the door to the Endicote's cabin swung back on its iron hinges and Saul and Joshua spilled out into the yard, wiping breakfast crumbs from their faces with a shirt sleeve. Following behind them, pulling for all his worth on Pharaohs lead was Kit. Once free of the cabin the hound scented the air and began barking. Reaching down, Kit slipped off his collar and watched, with more than a little longing, as the hound raced away and in the blinking of an eye, disappeared among the rows of corn.

Hearing the dog's bark, Shingas and Cattawa stopped in their tracks, alert and motionless. Dropping down onto one knee

Shingas pulled his knife from his sheath and waited expectantly. Within a matter of moments Pharaoh was on them, bounding forward, teeth bared, the hairs on the back of his neck bristling. With a malevolent snarl he leapt at Shingas' throat, flecks of saliva spraying from his open jaws. Instinctively, Shingas twisted his body sideways thrusting upwards with his knife as he did so, sinking its naked blade deep into Pharaoh's exposed chest. With a plaintive yelp the stricken hound fell onto the ground its snarl dying away to a whimper, its life blood draining away into the soil. When the dog's death throes had subsided, Shingas wiped the blood from his knife on its coat and pushed it back into its sheath.

Concerned that Pharaoh has suddenly stopped barking, Kit walked towards the cornfield and called out to him.

'Pharaoh. Here boy.' He waited a moment then called again. 'Here Pharaoh.'

Saul looked across at him, a grin spreading across his handsome face.

'Your hound has caught a rabbit little brother. He'll not come out till he's done eating his breakfast.'

Stung by his elder brother's words, Kit glared back at him angrily.

'He wouldn't do that, not my Pharaoh.'

Chuckling at Kit's show of temper, Saul and Joshua slung their muskets over their shoulders and ambled away towards the saw-pit.

Determined to prove Saul wrong, Kit strode towards the cornfield and called out again, louder this time.

'Here Pharaoh. Here boy.'

His patience exhausted, Kit clambered over the fence and ventured into the towering rows of corn in search of his hound.

Standing barefoot on a low stool, a garland of freshly picked wild flowers fixed in her auburn hair, Esther glanced down at Mrs Endicote kneeling at her feet, busy with needle and thread tacking up the hem of the long cambric dress she was wearing. All about her the room was in a clutter, the breakfast things still littered the table, the bed in the corner unmade and a pair of her bloomers, freshly washed, hung from the back of a chair airing in front of the fire. The dress had been Mrs Endicote's suggestion, indeed she had insisted on it. Determined that Esther should 'look the part' she had retrieved it from a large pine chest containing all that remained of her wardrobe. It was a fine dress with long fitted sleeves widening at the cuffs with two small buttons as decoration. A dress she herself had worn on many occasions, not least when attending church, so she had thought it fitting that it should be worn by Adam's bride on the day of his wedding. Suddenly the crash of musket-fire startled them both and abandoning her task, Mrs Endicote gripped the edge of the table and pulling herself up onto her feet, she hurried to the window and peered outside.

Shocked by the sound of gunfire Kit stood transfixed, his legs paralysed by fear. Moments later the terrifying sound of war-whoops coming from beyond the small cabin, assailed his ears. Rooted to the spot by uncertainty, the spell was broken when he saw the two Indians moving towards him along the row of corn, the sight of their painted faces striking terror into his heart. In an instant, all thought of his hound erased from his mind, he turned and fled back towards the cabin. Tomahawk in hand, Cattawa let out a whoop and moving with the grace of a panther he gave chase.

At the same moment, the cabin door swung open and Mrs Endicote rushed outside with Esther following a step behind her, the dress hiked up around her knees, the needle with its length of thread still hooked in the hem. Looking frantically about them, they caught sight of Kit as he raced out from the row of corn and began clambering over the fence.

Hauling himself up onto the top rail, Kit saw them and opened his mouth to shout out a warning. But before he could utter a sound, Cattawa was upon him and with a savage cry the young warrior brought his tomahawk down onto Kit's head, cleaving his scull almost in two with a single blow.

Mrs Endicote watched in horror as Cattawa raised his tomahawk and struck once more at Kit's head. Demented beyond reason by what she had witnessed, with a blood curdling scream, she snatched up the heavy wood-axe leaning against the chopping block and like an enraged Amazon she charged towards her son's killer.

Alerted by her agonising scream Cattawa released his grip on the tomahawk and leaving it embedded in Kit's head, he unslung his musket. Resting its long barrel on the fence rail he cocked the hammer and taking careful aim he pulled back on the trigger. The musket exploded and like a stricken animal, the lead ball lodged deep in her heart, Mrs Endicote's legs gave way and she sprawled lifeless onto the ground, the axe handle still gripped in her hands. At that same moment, Shingas appeared at the edge of the cornfield and spotting Esther, with the ease of an athlete he vaulted the fence and ran towards her.

Filled with terror, Esther turned and raced back towards the open door of the cabin. Reaching its safety, she slammed the heavy door shut and reached for the bolt. But just as her fingers closed around it the door burst inwards and she was thrown into the room and sent staggering back against the table, a scream welling in her throat as she saw Shingas framed in the doorway like some terrible apparition. Horrified, Esther leaned back against the table and as she did so her hand brushed against a knife. Instinctively she closed her fingers around its handle and as Shingas strode towards her, a look of triumph on his face, with a wild cry she raised the knife in the air and struck out at him. As the blade descended in one fluid movement Shingas reached up and grasped her wrist. A good head taller than Esther, he glared down into her eyes, slowly tightening his iron grip as he did so. Unable to bear the pain, Esther released her grip and the knife fell from her grasp and clattered onto the floor. Still gripping her by the wrist, Shingas dragged Esther from the cabin and out into the yard. Terrified out of her mind and fearing that at any moment she would be murdered, Esther's legs buckled under her and she sank to her knees, staring about her, wide-eyed with fear.

Whooping and yelling, Tusonderongue and the two young warriors, both with a plundered musket slung over their shoulder, ran out from the barn. All three were holding a flaming brand, a length of wood soaked in tar oil and set alight. Following behind them flapping and squawking, the hens made their escape through the open doors as flames licked hungrily at the stacked bales of hay engulfed in a smoking pool of fiery tar oil, which rippled outwards from the upturned barrel. Across from the barn the unfinished cabin was already ablaze, the bright orange flames, encouraged by the breeze which ran down the valley, rapaciously devouring its dry timbers and sending plumes of black smoke up into the air.

Shingas called out to them and pointed towards the cabin. Immediately the three warriors ran towards its open door and disappeared inside. Moments later their act of arson completed, they emerged and shrieking their war-cry, two of them threw their flaming brands up onto the bark roof of the cabin, whooping with delight when the dry, resin-rich shingles caught alight.

SHINGAS

Dragging Esther up onto her feet, with a shout Shingas gathered the war party around him and together they moved away from the cabin, where flames were already licking at the windows and taking hold on the roof. As they passed the saw-pit, Esther clutched a hand to her mouth and let out a strangled scream when she saw Saul's and Joshua's scalped bodies sprawled out in a gruesome repose beside the deep pit. Seizing her by the arm, Shingas dragged her away, past the cornfield and into the meadow beyond. Reaching the stream and leaving Esther standing on the bank, Shingas stepped into the fast flowing current and began washing the dog's blood from his hands and arm in its cold clear water.

Silently the four young warriors gathered about Esther studying her with child-like curiosity. Cattawa took a step towards her and attempted to lift up her skirt but Esther slapped his hand away. Piqued, Cattawa snatched the garland of flowers from her head and threw it onto the ground. Shingas watched the incident, admiring her spirit, then addressing the three warriors, his words spoken with authority, he turned away and splashed across to the far bank. Tusonderongue gestured for Esther to follow and pulling the hem of her dress up to her knees, she stepped into the brook and waded across to the other side. When all were across, with Tusonderongue leading the way, Esther and the war-party moved off through the tall grass towards the encircling wall of forest. Behind them smoke from the burning buildings rose upwards, a black smudge on the canvas of blue sky. Casting a last forlorn look over her shoulder, Esther turned away, overwhelmed by a flood of emotions. For now she was safe and alive but what lay ahead she could only contemplate with a sense of dread and foreboding.

With a crack of his whip Samuel urged the oxen into the river. Seated beside him and clearly not enjoying his bumpy outing was

Minister Rathbone. Behind them the cart was piled high with furniture, a wide pine table, several matching chairs and a large bed. Ahead of them Adam waded through the knee-high water eager to return to the farm and the ceremony that lay ahead. Suddenly he lifted his head and cried out, pointing as he did so to a distant column of black smoke rising above the tops of the trees ahead of them. Throwing aside the whip, Samuel snatched up his musket and jumping down from the cart he hurried after Adam who was already running along the track towards the blackening patch of sky.

Eventually the ox-cart lumbered into view with Minister Rathbone pulling uncertainly on the reigns, coming to an involuntary stop when, confronted by the terrible scene before him, he allowed the reigns to slip from his hands. The homestead was in ruins with flames still licking at the smouldering remains of its log walls. The cabin's roof had collapsed, engulfing the rooms below in the smouldering remains of shingles and beams, its stone chimney standing like an obelisk among the charred and blackened timbers. Much of the barn had been consumed by fire but miraculously the cow had survived, its calls to be milked somehow sounding incongruous. Lowering his gaze, he spotted Samuel kneeling on the ground with his dead wife tenderly cradled in his arms. Beyond him, Kit's lifeless body lay draped over the fence like a discarded coat. Suddenly Adam appeared, running in from the field, his cheeks wet with tears, his hand clutching the small garland of flowers. Reaching his father's side he dropped onto his knees.

'Esther is gone Pa. The savages have taken my Esther.'

Upon hearing Adam's plaintive words, Minister Rathbone dragged his eyes away from the scene of horror and devastation before him and shielding his face against the bright morning sun, he gazed out beyond the farm towards the forest, dark and foreboding in its primitive majesty. Unconsciously, his hand closed around the golden cross hung about his neck and his lips began moving in a silent prayer. A prayer for the living, the dead would have their turn when they were lowered into the earth.

CHAPTER SEVEN

WITH ONLY A narrow unfrequented trail to guide them, the war-party and their captive moved ever deeper into the seemingly unending wilderness of mountain and forest, an impervious wall of trunks and boughs blanketed by a dense canopy of leafy arches. Scorching in the hot June sun, pine-trees diffused the sultry air with their resinous odours and from some lofty perch the screech of a Red-tailed hawk was the only sound to intrude on the silence. Without rest and walking at a steady pace, they climbed up and over the backs of wooded hills and plunged through matted thickets, each step taking them farther away from the frontier settlements. By mid-morning with her bridal gown dirtied and torn by hard-beaked thorns, her bare feet cut and bloodied, Esther dropped to her knees gasping for breath, her body unwilling to take another step. In an instant Shingas was at her side, glaring down at her menacingly. Lifting her head Esther stared up at him beseechingly. Unmoved, Shingas thrust a hand into his carry-all and took out a length of rawhide rope. Seizing hold of Esther's arm he looped one end of the rope around her wrist and dragged her up onto her feet. With the rope clutched tightly in his hand he then turned away and leading her like a haltered animal, he set off again but this time at a slower pace.

Reaching a fast flowing stream, mercifully Shingas called a halt and letting go his grip on the rawhide rope he walked towards the stream. Freed of her restraint, with the last of her strength, Esther stumbled towards the low bank and throwing herself onto the ground, with cupped hands she ladled the clear, pure water into her mouth. With her thirst sated, she plunged her head into the stream, letting the waters flow through her dishevelled hair, the racing current cooling and invigorating.

After what seemed like only minutes Shingas took hold of her halter and they set off again into the virgin forest. Refreshed and with water running down her neck and dripping onto her shoulders, Esther hitched up the hem of her dress and not letting the rope tighten between them, she strode after him. Admiring her fortitude, the four young warriors fell in behind her and in moments they were all swallowed up once more by the gloomy woods.

After journeying for five more gruelling miles through the unforgiving forest, nightfall descended, enveloping them in darkness with surprising swiftness. Grateful for its arrival, each of the warriors sought out a bed among the trees and stretched out on the carpet of pine needles. With the rope untied from around her wrist Esther slumped onto the ground totally exhausted and curling herself into a ball, she was quickly asleep, her weary body cocooned in a cloak of comfort. Shingas stood over her for a moment, watching as sleep gently smoothed the rigours of the day from her face. He also looked at where the rawhide rope had left a raw welt around her wrist.

A cathedral hush pervaded the awakening forest and as the morning's light filtered through the canopy of leaves, the war-party left their night camp and with their guide Tusonderongue leading them, they made their way once more along the narrow path as it wound away into the depths of the encircling woods. Freed of her tether, Esther followed a pace behind Shingas with Cattawa and the other two warriors walking in single file behind them.

As they moved cautiously through the crowded trees, Tusonderongue suddenly threw up a hand and then pointed ahead of them to where a cluster of wigwams were just discernible through the foliage, with wisps of white smoke rising up into the chill morning air through their smoke-holes. As the war-party skirted around the Wyandot village the silence was rudely shattered by the wailing of a hungry baby. Thankfully before the noise woke the camp-dogs, its lusty cries were quickly silenced when it was given a breast to suckle.

Just beyond the village lay a vast lake, its gently rippling waters stretching away to the far horizon where a boundless panorama of forest covered mountains stood piled against the sky. Lying upturned on a sandy spit of land like seals basking in the sun were a dozen birch bark canoes. Instantly Cattawa and another warrior raced across to them and turning over two of the canoes, they dragged the frail craft down to the water's edge and set them afloat. Behind them Tusonderongue and the other young warrior took out their tomahawks and began hacking at the remaining canoes, smashing holes in their bottoms and rendering them useless.

With two warriors seated in each canoe, Shingas gestured to Esther and obediently she too climbed into one of the canoes and seated herself between the two rowers. After pushing both canoes off from the shore, Shingas waded out into the shallows and clambered aboard and with gentle strokes the two canoes glided out into the immense lake, its surface shimmering in the rays of the morning sun like an upturned mirror. High above them, a pair of fish-hawks circled lazily in ever widening spirals, wings outstretched, rising higher into the cloudless blue sky on the warming air, their shrill calls echoing in the natural amphitheatre.

Quickly the two canoes gathered speed, their curved prows cutting through the water in line abreast, the four Seneca warriors dipping and pulling their paddles in perfect time. Kneeling upright between the two rowers, thankful for the cooling breeze, Esther cast a despairing look at the receding shoreline, all hope of rescue fading with every stroke of the paddles.

Seated in the prow of the other canoe, when they reached deeper water, Shingas opened his carry-all and removed a length of fishing line. Attached to one end was a barbed hook with a silver lure shaped like a spoon and decorated with a kingfisher's wing-feather. Holding tightly to the other end of the line, he cast the lure into the water, letting out the line as it sank below the surface, spinning and flashing, iridescent in the clear water. In moments Shingas felt a tug on the line and hauling it in, hand over hand, he pulled a large lake trout clear of the water. Dropping his wriggling catch into the bottom of the canoe, he freed the hook from its mouth and cast the line out again. Watching him from the other canoe, Esther stared in fascination as the line jerked once more and Shingas hauled in an even bigger fish, the water running like mercury off its silvery scales.

When they were out of sight of the shore, the four warriors slowed the rhythmic pace of their paddling and allowed the canoes to glide across the glassy surface of the water with barely a ripple. So vast was the lake that to Esther it seemed like journeying across an ocean. The far shore lost somewhere beyond the horizon and despite her dire predicament she found herself lost in admiration at the majesty beauty which surrounded her. Eventually though, as the day progressed, without shade or shadow to protect her from the burning rays of the sun, her enjoyment waned and she was forced to splash handfuls of water from the lake onto her exposed skin. Occasionally a warrior would pause in his paddling to dip a cupped hand into the lake and slake his thirst. Parched with thirst, reluctantly Esther was forced to follow their example only to be amazed and surprised at how pure and pleasant the water tasted.

With the sun's golden orb sinking swiftly below the peaks of the distant mountains they at last reached the lakes southern shore. Jumping from their canoes the paddlers pulled them up onto a narrow sandy beach and dragged them out of sight among the low branches of the encircling trees. Without a word, Tusonderongue and another warrior disappeared into the forest in search of fire wood, returning a short time later, their arms filled with kindling and dry branches and in moments a smokeless fire was lit, the glow from its dancing flames radiating outwards. Seated beyond the expanding circle of light with her knees drawn up to her chest, her arms wrapped around them, Esther watched as Shingas and Cattowa carried the day's catch to the fire and began slitting open the bellies of the fish. After gutting them with the tip of their knives, they then skewered each fish in turn on a thin stick and lay them in the flames to cook. Like hungry children Tusonderongue and the two other warriors gathered about the fire, watching the flames work their magic.

Totally ignored, Esther looked on as the war-party feasted on the cooked fish, tearing the flaky white flesh from its spiny bones with their fingers and cramming it into their mouths. When they had eaten their fill, wiping their oily fingers on their breech-cloth they moved away from the fire and stretching out on the soft ground they quickly fell asleep.

With the sound of their slumber in her ears, famished, Esther crawled slowly on hands and knees towards the dying fire with the remains of the war-party's meal scattered on the ground around it. Suddenly, without warning Cattawa awoke and turning towards her he fixed her with his eyes, his stern expression unremitting. Transfixed, Esther stared back at him, her heart pounding like a drum. Seconds become a minute and then seemingly disinterested, Cattawa turned away, rolled onto his side and went back to sleep. Relieved, Esther seized her chance and like a feral cat she began scavenging among the discarded fish bones for morsels of food. Having gleaned a meagre supper, Esther returned to her sandy bed and laying on her back licking each of her greasy fingers in turn, she stared up in wonder at the inky black canopy of the night sky. A heavenly panorama, ablaze with the lights of distant worlds, some shining bright and steady like beacons, others flickering like celestial fireflies and in moments she was lost in sleep.

It was well into the morning before the war-party, led by Tusonderongue departed, moving away from the lake shore in their customary single file and entering once more into the silent bosom of forest. Earlier each warrior had removed several small leather pouches, each containing a different pigment, from their carry-all. After selecting a colour and moistening it with saliva they then mixed it into a paste, and with the tip of a finger began applying it to their faces, faithfully following the original pattern. With a fresh coat of war-paint applied Shingas produced a small fragment of mirror so that each warrior could admire his own handiwork.

Leaving the great lake behind them, the war-party moved deeper into the labyrinth of towering trees. With every yard Tusonderongue's pace seemed to lengthen and Esther, her last reserves of strength draining away, struggled to keep up. Unknown to her the war-party had entered the hunting grounds of the Seneca and with their village now within easy reach, the trail they were on was familiar to them, drawing them onwards like a beckoning finger.

Mercifully, reaching a small clearing, Shingas called a halt and with a great cry he raised his musket and fired it into the air. Immediately, whooping and yelling, the other warriors threw up their muskets and fired a ragged volley into the air, the sound reverberating through the dark canopy of branches. Done in, Esther dropped to her knees, gasping in lungs-full of air. Shingas looked across at his prisoner, then striding towards Esther, with a gesture of his hand he ordered her to get up. Climbing wearily to her feet, Esther stared back at him, her face etched with despair. One ordeal was almost over but ahead of her she knew lay another, more daunting even than the first and her heart sank at the thought of it.

CHAPTER EIGHT

ON THE SLOPING hillside beside the village, Meeataho and a group of squaws, each armed with a hoe moved among the rows of corn and squash tilling the rich soil. Some had babies in cradles strapped to their backs and despite the midday heat they chattered happily among themselves as they went about their work, occasionally erupting into fits of laughter when one of them chose to reveal some intimate secret or confess to an illicit dalliance.

Then without warning the crash of gunfire rolled in like the rumble of distant thunder. Immediately the squaws threw down their hoes and with Meeataho racing ahead of them, they ran squealing like excited children towards the village.

A crowd had already gathered on the fringe of the quadrangle and as Meeataho pushed her way through them she saw Shingas, head held high, striding purposefully through the village with Esther at his side. Following close behind him were the four Seneca warriors, each with a bloody trophy adorning their belts. In an instant an excited crowd gathered about them, clamouring for a sight of their captive. Meeataho stood watching from a distance, her expression one of bewilderment. Her heart had leapt when she caught sight of Shingas but when she had seen the white woman at his side, her blood had turned to ice.

Reaching the doorway to his long-house Shingas stopped. Immediately the jostling crowd fell silent, expectant. Sensing their mood, Shingas hesitated for a moment, then reaching out he pulled aside the curtain coving the entrance and taking hold of Esther's arm he pushed her inside. Instantly a great shout went up from the watching Indians, the white woman was to be Shingas' new wife. Impervious to the shouts from the excited crowd, Shingas turned and enveloped by the throng of people, he strode away towards the council lodge.

Dishevelled and dirty from her arduous journey Esther stood a little way in from the doorway and surveyed the building's gloomy interior. Its long central isle was empty apart from a number of fire-pits set at intervals along its length and down each side she saw what appeared to be compartments, much like the stalls of a stable and above them, suspended from the rafters in a golden tapestry, were ripened ears of maize.

Before she could contemplate what to do, the curtain at the doorway was pulled aside and Meeataho, her jet black eyes blazing with anger, stepped inside.

Esther stared at her, unsure as to what her appearance meant while at the same time conscious of the woman's apparent hostility towards her. Her uncertainty was quickly answered when with a wild cry Meeataho hurled herself at her, both arms outstretched, her fingers hooked into claws. Instinctively Esther reached out and grabbed Meeataho's wrists forcing her clawing fingers away from her face. Taking a step back Meeataho wrenched her hands free and with her teeth bared like some wild animal, she lunged forward and as their bodies come together, she grabbed handfuls of Esther's hair in both her hands and yanked her head back.

Desperately Esther retaliated by clutching handfuls of Meeataho's hair and pulling on it with all her might. Locked in this savage embrace the two women struggled back and forth until hampered by her long dress Esther stumbled backwards and the two women fell to the ground. With their fingers knotted in each other's hair they rolled around on the earthen floor, fighting like a pair of wildcats, each struggling to straddle the other. Gaining the upper hand Meeataho forced Esther onto her back and was just about to throw her leg across her and pin her to the ground, when with a wild shout Esther lashed out with her feet and sent Meeataho sprawling backwards.

Panting with exertion, both women clambered to their feet and with clumps of each other's hair trapped under their nails, their bodies bent forward at the waist, they begin circling each other warily like a pair of wrestlers. Sensing that her rival was tiring, Meeataho lunged forward eager to sink her claws into Esther's face and eyes. Without thinking, Esther reacted by standing upright and planting her feet slightly apart, she clenched her fists and with her arms raised and bent at the elbow like a bare-knuckle boxer, left arm forward of the right, she jabbed out her left arm like a piston and punched Meeataho in the face.

The blow struck Meeataho in the mouth and she staggered backwards, blood flowing down her chin from the gash in her lip. Regaining her balance, Meeataho wiped at her bloody lip with the back of her hand and then consumed with rage, she charged headlong at Esther. Fists tightly clenched, Esther waited until Meeataho was almost upon her and then she punched out her left arm. Instantly a stabbing pain shot down her arm as her knuckles connect with Meeataho's jaw, sending the young squaw sprawling backwards onto the ground.

Laying dazed on the ground Meeataho looked up at Esther expecting at any moment that she would fall on her. Instead, Esther stood motionless her arms dropped down at her side. Puzzled by her opponent's action Meeataho slowly pulled herself up onto her feet and staring at Esther with undisguised hatred, she reached down and pulled a knife from the belt around her waist, its exposed blade glinting in the half light. Gripped with fear Esther backed away her eyes full of dread. Desperately she looked about her for a way of escape but there was none. With a look of pure evil on her face, Meeataho flung back her mane of black hair and slowly advanced towards Esther, forcing her back until eventually she was trapped against the wall of the long-house. With a triumphant cry, Meeataho raised the knife in the air but before she can bring the blade down, the handle of a hoe suddenly appeared from out of nowhere and struck her hard across her shoulder. With a shriek of pain, Meeataho turned to face her attacker, watching in consternation as with a cackling laugh the old squaw lifted the hoe into the air again. Raising her arm to shield herself, the hoe struck her again and letting out an agonised cry, her fingers numbed by the blow, Meeataho let the knife slip from her grasp onto the dirt floor. Raising the hoe above her head once more, the old squaw shrieked with delight when she sees Meeataho run towards the doorway and disappear outside.

Looking pleased with herself the old squaw turned to Esther, her broad smile revealing a mouthful of decaying teeth and mimicking Esther's actions, she held up her bony arms and tightly clenched her fists.

Instantly, as though transported back in time, Esther found herself once more inside a large barn looking down from atop a huge crossbeam high up in its steeply pitched roof with a bird's eye view onto the floor below her. At the centre of this space was a small roped off square of ground surrounded by a dense crowd of men, cheering and baying like a pack of hounds. Inside the ropes, stripped to the waist, two bare-knuckle fighters stood toe to toe trading blows, neither willing to give an inch, their bodies glistening with sweat and splattered with flecks of each other's blood. One of the men was her father, a broad shouldered man with narrow hips and hands the size of sledge-hammers. The other fighter was much younger and quite handsome, despite the bloody swelling around his eyes where her father's brine soaked fists had pummelled them until they were almost shut. Both fascinated and disgusted in equal measures by the spectacle, she found herself unable, unwilling even, to leave and even as the revulsion grew within her she had stayed on and watched them fight. She also remembered with great clarity how later that same night, the young fighter, the blood washed from the cuts around his eyes and wearing a clean blue linen shirt, had carried her back to the barn in his strong arms. Remembered too how with unexpected tenderness, his rough hands, surprisingly gentle as they touched her face, neck and breasts, had seduced her and how although not yet sixteen on that warm summer night she had known a man for the first time.

The sound of the old squaw's voice, jabbering at her in a language she could only guess at, woke her from her reverie and staring back at her rescuer Esther shrugged her shoulders, she didn't understand. Grabbing hold of Esther by the wrist, the old squaw lead her over to the nearest fire, where a large stewpot, filled with a kind of porridge made from boiled maize and flavoured with berries and pumpkin seeds, hung over its low flames. Picking up an earthenware bowl, with her other hand the old squaw took hold of the swan-necked ladle, a prize plundered from some settlement kitchen, and after stirring it vigorously for a moment or two, she ladled a helping into the bowl and handed it to Esther. Ravenous, Esther lifted the bowl to her lips and eagerly scooped the porridge into her mouth with her fingers. With a satisfied look on her thin, wrinkled face, the old squaw looked on, the ladle still held in her hand, ready in case Esther should need a second helping.

Unable to cram anymore food into her mouth, Esther set down the bowl and in un-ladylike fashion, wiped the back of her hand across her mouth. Dropping the ladle back into the pot and gesturing for Esther to follow her, the old squaw made her way along the narrow aisle, stopping midway along, outside the open entrance to one of the partitioned rooms and pointing with a spindly finger, she indicated for Esther to go inside.

Stepping into the confined space Esther looked around her, taking in the strangeness of the compartment. The floor was made from bark planks set a few inches above the ground and covered by a coarse rush mat. Resting on them were two cots, each covered in animal furs and barely wide enough for two persons to sleep together on. Between these narrow beds, piled up against the back wall were wicker baskets, wooden trenchers and an assortment of earthenware pots. Turning to face the old squaw, Esther found to her amazement that she had gone and for the first time since her capture she realised that she was completely alone. Overwhelmed by the thought, exhausted, Esther slumped onto one of the cots, stretched out, and with her head cradled in the crook of her arm, she quickly fell asleep.

She was awoken after what seemed like only minutes by the sound of voices and for the briefest of moments her heart leapt. But then she realised that the voices she was hearing were speaking in a language which was alien to her. Flinging aside the animal's skin which she had pulled over herself, Esther swung her feet onto the rush mat and peering out through the opening she watched as Seneca families, mainly squaws and young children, moved down the aisle towards their own rooms. Many of them, especially the children, stole furtive glances as they passed, quickly looking away when Esther caught their gaze. Two young children, a boy and a girl, much bolder than the others, stood and stared in at her with mischievous curiosity. Moments later and a squaw called out, a note of authority in her voice and grinning like cats the pair turned and scampered away down the aisle. Alone again, Esther settled back onto the cot and surrounded by the sound of chattering voices, she closed her eyes, longing for sleep to come and rescue her from reality.

This time it was someone shaking her, which woke her and opening her eyes Esther gazed up to see the old squaw standing over her, a pair of beaded moccasins in one of her bony hands and what looked like a pole gripped in the other. Apprehensively, Esther climbed to her feet and immediately, without saying a word, the old squaw threw the moccasins onto the cot beside her and thrusting the pole into Esther's hand, she turned and walked away. Soon realising that what she held in her hand was in fact a hoe, with all thoughts of breakfast quickly forgotten, Esther hastily pulled on the moccasins, which fitted surprisingly well and with the hoe clutched in her hand she hurried after the old squaw. Once outside she caught up with the old woman and fell in beside her as she wove her way through the waking village.

When the pair reached the fields on the outskirts of the village, a dozen or so squaws were already at work, moving slowly down the rows of ripening corn busy with their hoes and chattering happily among themselves. A few had babies strapped to their backs in a cradle, their chubby faces smeared with bear oil, their enormous coal black eyes staring out at everything around them with innocent curiosity. For a moment the idyllic scene lifted Esther's spirits but then the old squaw's stern look reminded her that she was here to work. Selecting an untended row, Esther set to with her hoe, conscientiously working it into the rich soil, her mind focused on the work and taking what comfort she could from its distraction. On occasions when she stood up to stretch her aching back, she would catch sight of a squaw glancing at her, quickly averting her eyes when she saw that Esther had noticed her . As the morning wore on these moments became fewer and if she did happen to meet another squaw's gaze, more often than not they would exchange a smile.

With their work in the cornfield done, the group of squaws moved lower down the hillside to an area of open ground planted with squash and pumpkin. Before following them, desperate to relieve herself, Esther lingered behind and then with no one to see her, bundling up her dress, she squatted down and with no bloomers to contend with, she relieved herself.

Re-joining the other squaws and grateful for the touch of sunlight on her body, Esther unbuttoned the neck of her dress and began working again with her hoe, the old squaw never far away, a constant chaperone. Straightening for a moment to brush back her hair, she heard a young child call out and turning towards the sound, she watched in disbelief as from the far side of the field, a young girl of no more than six or seven, came running towards her. Even before the girl reached her, Esther could see from the paleness of her skin and the linen dress she was wearing, gathered at the waist and encircled by a wide leather belt with a plain brass buckle, that she was not a child of the Seneca.

Reaching the spot where Esther stood the child rushed up to her and flung her arms around Esther's legs calling out to her in a small pitiful voice. In total amazement Esther gazed down at the wretched girl's tear streaked face. Her hair was a mass of tangles and knots and her once pretty dress, soiled and stained and although she could not understand what the girl was saying, Esther knew immediately that the language she spoke was French. Dropping onto one knee, Esther took the young girl into her arms and hugged her to her, whispering softly to try and calm her. Around them an expectant hush settled over the watching squaws. Suddenly aware, Esther lifted her head and looking over the young girl's shoulder, she saw the reason for their silence.

Striding purposefully towards them, her face set hard, her black eyes flashing with anger was a burly squaw. Slowly Esther pushed herself up onto her feet, her hands instinctively clenching into fists. Catching sight of the squaw the young girl let out a scream and clutching tightly to Esther's dress with both hands she hid behind her, clearly terrified. Confronting Esther the burly squaw demanded in a guttural voice that the girl be returned to her, reaching out her hand as she spoke. Esther took a pace backwards and stooped down to retrieve her hoe. Again the burly squaw spoke, jabbing a finger at the young girl peering out at her from behind Esther's skirts. Slowly Esther shook her head. No! Incensed, the burly squaw took a step forward and reached out to seize the girl. In an instant Esther raised her hoe, threatening to strike her with it. Shocked by Esther's action the burly squaw quickly stepped back, angry but also a little uncertain. A sort of sigh rose from the watching squaws, half-shocked, half-excited and expecting that at any moment the two women would begin fighting, they gathered around them in a tight circle. The burly squaws name was Tekakwitha. Embittered by a childless marriage a month ago her husband had traded the French girl from a Shawnee war-party. But sadly the gift only served as a constant reminder to the squaw of her failure to bear children, and athough she was not cruel to the child she showed her little affection. Deciding what must be done, it was the old squaw who took matters in hand. Walking up to Esther she pointed at the locket hanging from the silver chain around her neck, and gestured for Esther to take it off. Realising what the old woman was suggesting, Esther immediate reaction was to refuse. Although the locket itself was of no real value, inside its ornamental case was a painted likeness of her mother, a woman she could barely recall except for a glimpse of her picture. Again the old squaw gestured with her finger, scolding her in a language she didn't understand but whose tone she did. Staring down at the wretched face of the young girl, Esther's resolve weakened and with a heavy heart she reached up and removed the locket from around her neck and meekly handed it to the old squaw.

Holding the silver chain between thumb and finger the old squaw dangled it enticingly in front of Tekakwitha while at the same time, with the persuasiveness of a snake oil salesman, she extolled its virtues as an amulet against sickness and witchcraft. Eventually, convinced by the old woman's rhetoric, Tekakwitha snatched the locket from her and slipped it into the small pouch hanging from her belt. As she did so a sigh went up from the watching squaws and the tension evaporated like a puff of smoke. Seemingly quite happy to have exchanged a child for a trinket, Tekakwitha then turned and made her way back to her corner of the field, and taking up her hoe once more she returned to her work.

With the woman gone, Esther knelt down in front of the young girl and smiling brightly she asked in a soft voice.

'What is your name?'

Immediately the girl's face dropped and she stared at Esther, clearly perturbed.

Sensing her disquiet, Esther reached out and took hold of one of her tiny hands and said in a voice filled with reassurance.

'Don't be afraid.'

Instantly the young girl stiffened and tried to pull her hand away, her crumpled face threatening to burst into a flood of tears at any second. As she did so, the old squaw stepped forward and scowling at Esther she pointed with her finger at the young girl, jabbering as she did so.

'Elle est Francaise! Francais!'

Although in ignorance of the words, Esther understood their meaning and was instantly aware of how devastated the child must be to find that her rescuer was not French as she had assumed and how disconcerting the sound of her voice must be to the child. With no other course open to her, Esther reached out and took the young girl into her arms and embraced her. For better or worse she was hers now, whether as a younger sister or as an adopted child she wasn't sure. What she was certain off was that despite the fact that they both spoke a different language, they were irrevocably bound together by their circumstances and by the colour of their skin. Looking on, her face creased into a rare smile, the old squaw cackled with pleasure, for it was not every day that one became a surrogate grandmother.

The next morning saw them back in the fields again, Esther busy with her hoe, the French girl beside her like a shadow. Last evening each had made an effort with their appearance. Seated in their room, the old squaw had produced a pot of bear grease and a porcupine comb from her bag of tricks and despite the child's howls of protest, Esther had set about combing the rats-tails of tangles from her shoulder length mousy brown hair. She had thought to plait it but deciding that her new charge had endured enough, instead she applied a small amount of the bear grease, working it into the child's mane of hair with her fingers until it shone like strands of copper wire. A scrub with a wetted cloth revealed a rounded sunburnt face with a pert little nose and large cerulean eyes (set just a little too far apart for a portrait painters liking). But what saved her face from plainness were her perfect butterfly lips, as pink as a wild rose. Esther too had combed the tangles from her own matted hair and done her best to repair the tears in her dress much to the supposed delight of the old squaw who hovered over the pair like a brothel mistress, pointing a finger at a missed tangle or a tear not stitched together to her liking.

Later in the morning a group of young children appeared on the a strip of open ground running alongside the cornfield and after dividing themselves up into two opposing teams, a ball the size of a baby's head, made from animal skin, stuffed with wadding and weighted with pebbles was produced and a game of 'catch and keep' began with the players of one team passing the ball to each other while the opposing team did all it could to steal it from them. Suddenly a pass was dropped and in an instant, shrieking with excitement, children from both teams threw themselves onto the ground, scrambling to retrieve the ball. Standing apart from the melee, a young girl spotted the French girl watching them and waving her arm she beckoned to her. Unsure, the French girl moved closer to Esther and took hold of her dress. She was not confident enough yet to let go of her new mother's apron strings. Seeing her reluctance, with a shrug of her shoulders the Seneca girl turned away and re-joined the game. Witnessing the incident, Esther placed her hand on the young girl's head, a touch which said 'it's all right'. Turning her back on the rough and tumble game, Esther caught sight of a young squaw with a baby strapped to her back on a cradle-board, looking across at her. Instinctively, she threw her a warm smile and was overjoyed when the young squaw smiled back. She was accepted.

Even before she swung her feet onto the rush mat floor Esther knew her period had started. With all that had happened, she had given little thought to its onset. Usually she was careful about their timing for such a thing was important in her relationship with Saul, only letting him lay between her legs when she knew that for all his thrusting, she would not conceive a child. Uncertainly she got to her feet, gritting her teeth against the stabbing pain in her belly, her face contorted into a grimace. Impatient to be off and unaware of Esther's condition, the French girl took hold of her hand and pulled her towards the aisle. Unsure of what to do Esther hesitated, gripping the corner post for support as another sharp pain knifed through her lower abdomen. She wanted to tell her to wait a moment but knew she wouldn't understand. Suddenly, like a genie from a bottle the old squaw was there, standing in front of her. Sensing something was wrong, the old squaw stared at Esther for a moment with hooded eyes, then stepping forward she gripped the hem of Esther's dress and pulled it up over her knees. Stooping down she peered up between Esther's legs and saw the trickle of blood running down the inside of her thigh. Filled with embarrassment, Esther stared down at her, her cheeks filling with colour.

Without a word the old squaw let go of the skirt and quick as a wink she was gone, returning moments later clutching an old trade blanket. Taking hold of Esther by the wrist, she pulled her from the small room into the aisle and then out through the long-house doorway. With an agility that belittled her age, the old squaw led Esther through the groups of squaws making their way to the fields and through the ordered rows of long-houses until they reached a small isolated birch bark building at the edge of the village. Constructed in the same manner as the other long-houses, it differed only in size, being just as wide but less than a third of the length. Without a word, the old squaw thrust the trade blanket into Esther's hands, pulled aside the curtain at the doorway, and pushed her inside. The French girl tried to follow but the old squaw grabbed her by the hand and dragged her away, muttering to her in a mixture of Seneca and French which, judging by the woeful expression on her face the child had no understanding of, save perhaps for the words 'Non' and 'La Femme' which the old woman repeated several times over.

Even before her eyes became accustomed to the building's gloomy interior, the thing which struck Esther first, was the overwhelming stench of unwashed bodies and the cloying reek of bodily odours, hanging like an invisible veil in the airless building. Knowing immediately from the smell and her own condition that what she had entered was a menstruation lodge, Esther quickly clamped a hand across her nose and mouth and quietly surveyed its interior. Beneath its over-arching roof, the building comprised of a large single room without divisions or compartments, the only light entering through a single smoke-hole in the roof.

In the centre of the dirt floor was a fire-pit and lining three of the walls were low cots on which several squaws in various stages of undress sat or sprawled out on, each with a blanket pressed between their thighs. For all its openness and lack of privacy a feeling of intimacy prevailed. Squatting on rush mats spread out around the fire smoking their short stemmed pipes, the clouds of sweet smelling smoke helping to mask the impurities seeping from their pores in the clammy heat of the building, were a small group of squaws. Each listening enthralled as one of the group, a buxom squaw, the top of her doeskin dress pulled down around her waist, her large pendulous breasts with protruding nipples the size and colour of a ripened acorn, on display for all to see, recounted the intimate details of a recent sexual liaison.

Becoming aware of Esther's presence, the buxom squaw fell silent and Esther suddenly felt every squaw's eyes fall on her, their curious stares stripping her bare. Eventually after what seemed like an eternity they seemed to lose interest and without a word being said, the moment passed. Turning her back on Esther the buxom squaw returned to her story, finishing the licentious tale by holding up a little finger in a derogatory pose. Shrieking with laughter her audience pressed her for more. Taking advantage of the distraction, Esther moved swiftly across to one of the cots and finding a vacant spot alongside two very young squaws, barely in their teens, huddled together like Siamese twins, she sat down and as discreetly as possible, she lifted the front of her dress and pushed the blanket up between her thighs.

SHINGAS

By the third day Esther's appreciation of the building and its function, in spite of the squalid conditions, had improved to the point where, like all the other squaws, she found that being an inmate, while not pleasant, was at least an escape from the everyday toils and tasks which were a squaws lot. Food and drink were brought to them and nothing more it seemed was expected of them, other than to idle away their time until their Menses had stopped. Even the two teenage squaws seemed happier with their lot. Having been befriended by an older squaw they spent much of their time busy decorating a leather pouch with coloured beads and lengths of porcupine quill.

With the upper half of her dress pulled down around her waist, her face, arms and small rounded breasts glistening with sweat, intrigued by the game being played amongst the squaws seated around the fire, Esther got up from her cot and crossed to the fire-pit. Seating herself on one of the rush mats and with her elbows resting on her knees, her chin propped up between her slender outstretched fingers, she began watching with interest as the buxom squaw and another squaw competed in a hand game. Totally absorbed, Esther quietly studied the rudiments of the game, while also observing the tactics and strategies employed by each player to outwit her opponent.

Each player had three disc shaped markers made from hardened clay, each one a slightly different shape from the others. Two were painted black the other painted white. With the three markers clutched in one hands, on a signal from the buxom squaw, the two squaws then clapped their hands together and clenching them into fists they put them behind their backs. Hidden from their opponents sight, each then moved their markers from one hand to another into their desired sequence. For a moment the two poker-faced players stared into each other's faces as though searching for a clue as to which hand the other would open and what it would hold. Finally, on a shout from the buxom squaw, both players held out their hands. As she had issued the challenge, the buxom squaw unclenched her right fist and revealed a white marker laying in the centre of her palm. With a despairing groan the other squaw opened both her hands, in one lay a black marker and in the other a black and white marker. A cry went up from the watching squaws, the buxom squaw has won the game. Disgruntled, the other squaw threw down her markers in disgust and getting to her feet, she walked away.

Smiling with pleasure, the buxom squaw reached down and scooped up the small pile of beads, her winnings from the game. Seeking another opponent, she then cast her gaze over the circle of squaws seated around the fire. Seeing Esther, she pointed a finger at the discarded markers and with a knowing look, invited her to pick them up. Filled with curiosity, more squaws crowded around the fire, watching with mounting interest as leaning forward, Esther picked up the three discarded markers. The challenge had been accepted. A smile flickered across the buxom squaw's face and filled with confidence, she pointed at the buttons on Esther's dress, identified them as acceptable to her as Esther's wager. Fingering each of the four pearl buttons in turn, Esther nodded her head in agreement. Satisfied, the buxom squaw matched Esther's bet by throwing down the pile of beads she had just won, onto the mat in front of her.

Facing the buxom squaw across the fire, Esther picked up the discarded markers and tracing each of their outlines carefully with her finger, she committed to memory the shape associated with each colour. Finally satisfied, she settled all three markers into the palm of her left hand and looked across at her opponent. She was ready. With a shout, the buxom squaw clapped her hands together and clenching them into fists, she hid them behind her back. Esther followed suit and both sat staring at one another across the glowing embers of the fire. Quick as a flash, the buxom brought her hands to the front and with a disdainful smirk on her face, she unclenched her left fist to reveal her white marker. Slowly, Esther uncurled the fingers of her left hand and also revealed a white marker. The watching squaws oohed admiringly, Esther had beaten the buxom squaw's challenge, it was a good start and now it was her turn.

Later that evening, taking advantage of the gathering darkness, Esther and two other squaws, their periods over, slipped out of the menstruation lodge. Skirting the outlying long-houses they made their way along the banks of the stream as it meandered around the foot of the low hill. Reaching a spot downstream of the village where its shallow waters flowed over and between outcrops of rock the two squaws dropped to their knees and began washing their blankets. Following their example, Esther crouched down and dipping her blanket into the cold, clear water she began scrubbing it with her hands, watching as the stream's murmuring wavelets were turned red by the dissolving blood.

With the blanket, still wet from its soaking, clutched in her hand Esther made her way to her long-house and hoping not to be noticed she drew back the curtain at its doorway and stepped inside. A golden glow enveloped the building as the light from the cooking fires dotted at intervals along the central isle reflected upwards onto the rows of ripened corn hanging from the rafters above. Seated together in their rooms, families ate their evening meal and talked in low voices. From somewhere a mother began singing a lullaby to her tired child. Everywhere a mood of harmony prevailed.

Suddenly a joyful cry rang out and with a smile as wide as her face, the French girl ran down the aisle towards her and flinging her arms around Esther's legs, she clung to them like a limpet. With her hopes dashed, Esther stooped down and taking the young girl into her arms she hugged her to her chest, feeling her own heart beating faster, like a mother's would when reunited with her child.

Freeing herself from the child's grip, Esther looked up and saw the old squaw hovering over them, staring down at her with piercing coal black eyes. Straightening, Esther held out the still damp blanket, muttering her thanks even though she knew the old woman would not understand. With a curt nod of the head the old squaw took it from her, running her eyes over Esther as she did so and tut- tutting at her dishevelled appearance and the soiled state of her dress. Blushing with embarrassment Esther brushed back a lock of hair, which had fallen across her face, while at the same time reaching up with her other hand and pulling together the button-less neck of her dress. Muttering something indistinguishable under her breath, the old squaw turned and walked away. Disappearing into one of the rooms, she re-emerging moments later with a doeskin dress, its neck and sleeves beautifully decorated with coloured beads, draped over her arms. Without a word, her face giving nothing away, she walked up to Esther and held out the dress. Hesitating briefly, Esther reached out and took it from her, amazed at how soft and light it felt in her hand and smiling warmly she nodded her head in gratitude.

No sooner had Esther received the gift when Shingas strode into the long-house and came and stood beside her. Shocked by his sudden appearance, this was the first time he had entered the long-house since bringing her to the village, seeing him again, struck fear into her heart and instinctively she shrank away from him. Shingas stared at her menacingly for a moment and then turned his gaze on the French girl, a frown transforming his face. Turning to the old squaw he said something to her, a hard edge to his voice. The old squaw stared back at him and with a haughty tilt of the chin she replied in a strong voice, saying only a few words but each one imbued with matriarchal authority. It was at that moment, in seeing the look which passed between them, that Esther sensed that this kindly old squaw might well be the mother of this savage who had abducted her. No sooner had the thought struck her when, taking her arm in a grip that made Esther wince, the old squaw lead her away.

As they walked away, Shingas stood for a moment as though caught in two minds, then he turned his gaze on the French girl once more, this time his expression was almost benign. Meeting his gaze the child put aside her fear and rewarded him with a small smile. With the hardness returning to his face, Shingas turned away and entered the compartment, seating himself cross-legged on one of the low cots, lost under a layer of furs. Moments later Esther appeared in the entrance carrying a crude trencher piled with food; strips of roasted meat still hot from the fire, boiled ears of corn and a flat loaf of unleavened bread. Stepping inside she set down the meal on the rush mat in front of Shingas and took a step back. Picking up a piece of freshly cooked meat between his fingers, with his other hand Shingas gestured for Esther to sit down. Obediently she seated herself on the cot opposite him, the French girl squatting down beside her. Cramming the piece of the meat into his mouth, Shingas looked across at Esther and nodded towards the trencher of food. Nervously, Esther picked up a few morsels of meat and an ear of corn and handed them to the French girl. Then tearing off a corner of the loaf and helping herself from what remained of the meat, with a quick smile at the girl, she began eating. Outside, unnoticed in the shadowy aisle, the old squaw peered in at the scene of domesticity, a self-satisfied smile spreading across her wrinkled face.

Late into the night, satisfied that Shingas was lost in a deep sleep, taking great care not to wake the sleeping child, and with the doeskin dress clutched under her arm Esther slipped out of the cot and guided more by memory than light, she left the small compartment and made her way to the doorway of the long-house. Pulling aside the curtain she stepped outside into a warm, moonlit night and familiar with the path she must take, Esther made her way through the cluster of long-houses. Reaching the edge of the cornfield Esther made her way down the gently sloping hillside towards the stream which lay at its feet, the ever changing sound of its purling waters carried up to her on the wings of the night air.

Quickening her pace, in moments she reached its grassy bank and stood gazing down as the wild stream snaked its way around the base of the hill, its current running deep and fast, its rippling surface, burnished by the lustre of a silver moon. Neatly folding the doeskin dress, Esther laid it down on the bank and then reaching down she grasped the hem of her dress with both hands and pulled it up over her head. Bathed in illuminant moonlight, she stood for a moment, gazing down at the alabaster texture of her exposed skin, marvelling at its whiteness when contrasted with her sunburned arms. With a smile touching her lips, the dress clutched tightly in her hand, Esther stepped into the stream. Feeling for a footing on the smooth pebbly bed the current swirling around her naked body with tentative steps, she waded further out away from the bank. Reaching mid-stream, with the water at waist height, Esther took a deep breath and bending her knees she slowly lowered herself until her whole body was completely submerged with only the long amber tresses of her hair visible in the flow of crystal clear water, rippling out like silken threads of eelgrass. Surfacing, she gulped in a mouthful of air and then immersed herself once more. She was under for some time, then gasping for breath she thrust up through the surface, exhilarated. Pushing the strands of wet hair from her face, a sudden movement caught her eye and turning her head towards it, she saw Shingas standing at the water's edge, silent as a statue, watching her, his unblinking gaze fixed on her naked body.

Instinctively Esther clutched the dress to her breasts, hiding her nakedness from him. But the gesture came too late and as she watched, Shingas stepped into the stream and moved towards her, the desire in his hooded eyes unmistakable. Terrified Esther backed away, the dress pressed against her chest, her other arm held out, the palm of her hand held up like a shield. She stumbled and almost went under but managed to recover her footing. Resolute, Shingas closed on her, impervious to the rush of water tugging at his legs. Despairingly Esther looked across towards the opposite bank, so near yet so far away.

In an instant Shingas was on her. Reaching out he took hold of her arm, his fingers gripping her soft flesh like a vice. Esther wanted to shout out but the scream died in her throat. Pulling on her arm, Shingas dragged her to the far bank and pushed her down into the shallows. Laying on her back in the ankle deep water, her arms outstretched, Esther watched in horror as the dress slipped from her grasp and like a thief in the night, the strong current plucked it from the eddying pool and carried it away downstream. With despairing eyes Esther followed its dipping, darting progress and her heart leapt when it snagged on a half-submerged rock. But just when her hopes were given new life, the capricious stream tugged it free and caressed by its swirling waters, the dress was carried off into the darkness. Tearing her eyes away, Esther looked up at Shingas towering over her, tall and menacing. With a low grunt he reached down to take hold of her. Instinctively Esther lashed out with her feet, fear and anger surging through her brain, each emotion the equal of the other. Avoiding her flailing legs, Shingas dropped to his knees beside her and seizing her arm and shoulder in his powerful hands, he forced her over onto her stomach, pushing her down until her head was under the water. With his quarry subdued, Shingas gripped each of Esther's legs just below the backs of the knee and wrenched them apart. Helpless, Esther lifted her head up out of the water and gasping for air she struggled to free her trapped arms. With his prize exposed, Shingas clamped a hand on the rounded cheeks of Esther's naked buttocks and pushing forward he forced her up onto her knees. Sensing his intention, with both her arms now freed, Esther lunged forward, stretching them out, her hands grabbing at the grassy bank, her clawing fingers striving for a handhold. Instantly a searing pain burned through her scalp as Shingas grabbed a handful of her hair and yanked her head back.

Subdued and helpless like a tethered animal, Esther winced, more from shock than pain when fully aroused, Shingas pulled aside his breech-cloth and plunged his engorged manhood into the enveloping softness of her ever open wound. Silently Esther endured his urgent, ever quickening thrusts, numbing her mind as he took his pleasure, thankful that she could not see his terrifying face and willing this defilement of her body to end. Mercifully in minutes her ordeal was over as grunting with exertion Shingas reached a shuddering climax and with a deep groan he released his grip on her hair and fell back onto his heels, his chest heaving as he sucked air into his lungs.

On all fours, hardly daring to move, not even to turn her head, Esther waited until she was sure that Shingas had gone, waited until his splashing steps had faded and the tranquil babbling of the stream prevailed. Only then did she push herself upright onto her knees and lift her head towards the starless sky. Tentatively, she reached a hand up between her thighs and touched herself, her fingers brushing the soft bush of hair between her legs and feeling his sticky semen. Filled with a sense of disgust, Esther moved a little way out into the stream and lowering herself into the water she stretched out full length, her back resting on its pebble bed, her feet pointing into the racing current. With her face just visible above the surface, her arms and legs spread wide like the points of a star, Esther lay on the bed of the stream like a fallen angel, praying that the shimmering waters flowing over the contours of her outstretched body would cleanse and purify it.

Next morning, wearing her new doeskin dress, Esther made her way to the fields, grim faced, staring straight ahead, failing even to acknowledge the admiring glances of the other squaws. Sensing something was amiss the French girl walked along beside her in silence, glancing up occasionally to see if Esther's expression had softened, only to be disappointed on each occasion.

Reaching the cornfield, the French girl spotted a group of children playing a game with wooden hoops and with a skip and a jump she ran across to join them. Esther watched her run off, pleased that she was to be left alone and hoe in hand she set about her work, driving her hoe into the hard ground as if she were chopping the head off a snake, quite oblivious to the squaws working alongside her, chattering happily among themselves.

Suddenly there was a commotion at the far side of the cornfield and crying out in alarm several squaws ran out from the rows of corn as though chased by the devil himself. Turning to see what had caused the disturbance, Esther was amazed when a horse suddenly burst out into the open and stood trembling and wild-eyed at the edge of the cornfield. Staring in disbelief, Esther laid down her hoe and without knowing why, save for a sense that it was what she must do, she slowly walked towards the frightened animal, noticing as she drew closer to it, just how thin and emaciated it was.

Alerted by the cries from the squaws, Pahotan and a number of warriors ran out from the village, stopping yards from the cornfield and staring in disbelief at the apparition before them. They knew it was the trader's horse, the same horse, which had carried their dead brother back to the village. But how had it survived? Time and time again they had driven it off into the forest, knowing that eventually some wild beast would devour it. Yet here it was, half-starved but alive. Turning to one of the warriors, Pahotan said something to him and immediately, the warrior handed Pahotan his musket. Cocking the weapon, Pahotan brought it up to his shoulder and aimed its long barrel at the horse.

With a desperate cry Esther rushed forward and interposed herself between Pahotan and the horse, crying out in a loud voice.

'No! No don't shoot! Please don't shoot.'

Perplexed, Pahotan hesitated and seizing the moment, Esther snatched up an ear of ripened corn from the pile they had harvested earlier that morning and stripping away the dry husk she walked towards the horse talking softly to it, her hand filled with corn held out in front of her. Instinctively the horse shied away pawing at the ground with a front hoof. Esther stopped, waited a moment for it to settle then moved forward again, her voice calm and reassuring. Eventually hunger prevailed and the starving horse took the offering of corn from the palm of her hand, grinding it between its blackened teeth. While it ate, Esther cast her eyes over the animal, wincing at the sight of the sores on its back and shoulders and the mat of blood-sucking ticks infesting its ears. Preoccupied, Esther was taken by surprise when the French girl suddenly appeared at her side, her small cupped hands filled with corn. Fearlessly and speaking to the animal in a language only she could understand, the young girl stepped up to the horse and held out her arms, cooing with delight when it ate from her hands. Looking on, the crowd of squaws awed with admiration at the child's boldness. Having done all she could to prove how harmless the creature was, Esther turned to Pahotan, hoping that he had got the message. Pahotan glared back at her, clearly not happy. Then slowly he lowered the musket and handing it back to the warrior he had taken it from, he shouted something contemptible to the squaws and turning on his heels he stalked off towards the village. Instantly news of the wild animal and how the young girl had tamed it, spread through the village. Within hours all fears of the horse were forgotten and within days, thanks to Esther's ingenuity, its place in the village was secure.

From the moment that the horse had taken the corn from her outstretched hand Esther had known that the animal held her only hope of escape. Freedom not just for herself but for the girl too for she could no sooner leave her behind than she could a daughter or sister. So with regular feeds of corn, sometimes boiled and pulped into a mash, something Esther had seen farmer Endicote do when the cow got sick the horse's condition improved. Esther also discovered that as well as its cosmetic qualities, a liberal amount of bears grease, applied as a salve, was also an effective cure for the animal's mangy sores. But what truly ensured the young mare's survival and their hope of escape was that while the squaws, old and young still had to forage in the forest for firewood, they no longer had to strap it to their backs and carry it to the village. Esther had seized on the opportunity and now she and the French girl had become a common sight, returning every day from the forest, the horse laden down with firewood, their comings and goings now part of the everyday life of the village.

Late one afternoon as Esther and the French girl unloaded the firewood onto the pile at the edge of the quadrangle, Esther noticed that they had an audience. With the last log thrown onto the wood-pile Esther turned to the small group of watching children and with a wave of her arm she beckoned them to her. With excited cries the children, boys and girls rushed across to her and one by one she lifted them up onto the horse's back where they clung to each other grinning like monkeys. Taking up the lead-rope Esther led the horse with its cargo of happy urchins away towards the edge of the village. As they walked between the rows of long-houses squaws, including some who's child was up on the horse's back, looked on with happy, smiling faces.

As they neared the stream Esther's attention was drawn towards an open patch of ground occupied by a group of older boys and girls standing in two ranks facing each other. Some she saw, mainly the girls, were each holding a stick in their hands. Suddenly a boy, who had been standing off to one side began running towards them. Drawing near he stopped for a moment and then lowering he head, he gave a shout and dashed forward along the open space between the two ranks. Surprised by the boy's strange behaviour, Esther was horrified when shouting and yelling, the two ranks of children struck at him with their fists and sticks. Her heart missed a beat, when half-way along the row, a heavily build youth swung out his arm and clubbed the boy across the head. Stumbling, the boy almost went down but regaining his momentum he charged on and with a final surge he emerged from the gauntlet with nothing worse than a trickle of blood running down from his nose.

Whooping with delight the ranks of children crowded around him, fists and stick exchanged for jubilant shouts of unadulterated joy. Filled with a sense of unease, Esther turned away and pulling on the lead-rope she led the horse down to the stream the sound of their noisy voices quickly fading away.

Standing knee-deep in the water while the horse slaked its thirst, filled with a sudden taste for mischief, Esther bent down and scooping up handfuls of the cold water, she began splashing it over the children clinging onto the horse's back. Smiling with delight when they shrieked with alarm at their drenching. On the opposite bank unseen among the overhanging trees, Shingas watched as again and again Esther soaked the screaming children with water. Touched by the scene of innocent pleasure, for a brief moment the iron mask of inscrutability slipped from his face and his hard features softened as he revelled in the children's enjoyment and bathed in the radiance of Esther's smile.

And so the days passed and became weeks and the horse grew stronger, its muscles and tendons strengthened by the heavy work, its glossy coat a testament to the healthy diet of corn and hay and Esther's healing lotions. But as the horse grew stronger so too did Esther's impatience but she was wise enough to know that the time had to be right, that the chance she had hoped and prayed for, when it came, must not be wasted. And so she waited, waited and prepared for that day to arrive.

When it came, it came unexpectedly, almost as if someone had waved a magic wand and cried abracadabra. Shingas had left his bed before dawn, slipping away from their room without a sound and later that morning, the old squaw, together with most of the village's squaws, each carrying a woven basket, had ventured off into the forest to harvest wild berries.

Returning to the village with their first load of firewood, helped by the French girl Esther stacked the logs and dry branches into a pile. A short distance away, half a dozen warriors lounged in the shade of a building, gossiping and smoking their pipes, totally at ease. Leading the horse to the entrance to her long-house, Esther slipped inside, returning moments later with a well-filled satchel slung across her shoulder. Glancing furtively at the group of warriors, she lifted the French girl up onto the horses back and with a last look over her shoulder she led it away, willing herself to walk at a slow pace.

Moving through the crowded trees with the skill of a seasoned hunter, the young warrior shadowed the group of squaws. Among them were several young maidens and one in particular had caught his eye. Edging closer, taking care not to be seen, the young buck looked longingly at the object of his desire, drooling as she bent over and plucked a handful of fruit from a blueberry bush, her dress tightly stretched across the perfectly formed contours of her body. Aware of his attention, the young maiden turned her face towards him and encouraged him with a coquettish smile.

Having plundered the bushes of their fruit, the group of berry-pickers walked deeper into the forest. Watching them move away, surreptitiously, the young maiden distanced herself from them, casting a sly look over her shoulder to see if he was still following. She need not have worried, her smile had been enough to seal his fate and with ardour burning like a fire in his belly, he shadowed her as she slipped between the trees supposedly in search of more berries. When the other squaws had disappeared out of sight, the young maiden turned and fixing him with her dark liquid eyes, she smiled at him again, bolder this time. The young buck hesitated for a moment and then finding his courage he strode eagerly towards her. With her trap sprung, the young maiden gave a teasing laugh and dropping her basket to the ground, not caring that half its contents spilled out, she slipped away into the trees. Determined not to let her escape, the young buck gave chase and though she ran with the fleetness of a deer, with every stride he gained on her. Suddenly she stopped and turned, facing him like a cornered, defenceless animal, her breathing deep and heavy, her chest rising and falling as she sucked in air through parted lips.

With his throat dry with passion, the young buck lunged for her. With a quick laugh, spinning on her heels, she evaded him with the skill of a matador. Single-minded, he closed on her his arms held out eager to clutch her to him and make her his. With a look akin to triumph the young maiden threw herself down onto her back and pulling up her dress, she showed herself to him. Dizzy with lust, the young buck looked down at the prize that awaited him. Then suddenly something distracted him, some movement among the trees caught his eye and turning away he saw them. Esther and the French girl up on the horses back, moving at an easy canter through the forest. A look of concern clouded his young face, then resolute he turned away and running as swiftly as he could he sprinted away, back towards the village. Lying abandoned on the ground, totally bemused by his actions, the rejected maiden stared after him, her fists clenched, her eyes blazing with anger.

Panting for breath, the young buck ran into the village and seeing Tusonderongue and a group of warriors sprawled on rush mats outside one of the long-houses he raced up to them and stumbling over his words, gave them his news. Jumping to his feet, Tusonderongue took the young buck aside and questioned him. Was he sure of what he had seen? The young buck nodded his head emphatically, yes what he had told them was true. Turning away, Tusonderongue strode across to the council-building and pulling aside the curtain he ducked inside. Filled with uncertainty the young buck waited, doubt clouding his mind. Should he have told them what he had seen? Had he acted too hastily? Before he had time to answer his own questions, Tusonderongue emerged with Shingas following behind him, his face like thunder.

Approaching the young buck, Shingas' features softened and when he spoke there was no anger in his voice.

'You saw them? The Yenge woman and the child.'

'Yes and the horse also, running fast.' He spoke the words boldly for it was the truth.

'Show me which way.'

The young buck half turned and reaching out his arm, he pointed in the direction that Esther had taken.

As a gesture of thanks, Shingas placed a hand on the young Indian's shoulder and squeezed it firmly with his fingers. Then without another word Shingas walked across to his long-house and disappeared inside, re-appearing moment later, with his musket clutched in his hand, and his carry-all and powder horn slung across his shoulder. Tusonderongue looked at him enquiringly. Shingas shook his head no, he would go alone. He must be the one to bring them back.

The horse moved swiftly through the forest, the drumming of its hooves like a muffled heartbeat. Up on its back Esther clung to the animal's mane with one hand kicking its flanks with her heels, urging it on. Sitting behind her, with both arms wrapped tightly around Esther's waist, the French girl clung on, her face buried in Esther's back to avoid the swishing branches as they plunged ahead through the trees.

Jogging at a pace he could maintain for half a day, Shingas slipped through the trees, following the horse's hoof-prints like a hound on a scent, the heavy musket slung across his shoulder. A mile ahead of him, pulling on the lead rope she had improvised into a rein, Esther slowed the tired animal, its neck lathered with sweat, its sides heaving, to a walk. Up behind her the French girl relaxed her hold on Esther's waist, thankful for the temporary respite from the jolting ride. Sensing the child's relief, Esther turned her head and smiled at her reassuringly.

Shingas had been running for two hours but he showed no sign of tiredness. Suddenly ahead of him he caught a glimpse of the horse with Esther and the French girl astride it. Quickening his pace he began gaining on them with every stride.

Without knowing why, some sixth sense perhaps, the French girl threw a look over her shoulder and instantly saw Shingas running through the crowded trees towards them. Opening her mouth she screamed, the noise deafening in the sepulchral silence of the woods. Shocked by the sound, Esther spun around and instantly saw the reason for it. Instinctively, she kicked at the horse, urging it into a run. But Shingas was up with them now, matching the horse stride for stride. Reaching out an arm he clutched at the girls leg. Shrieking in terror she pulled it away from his grasping hand. Esther kicked again at the horse, digging her heels into its sides, leaning forward across its neck, shouting to it, urging it on. The horse responded, its powerful legs pumping like pistons, its hooves digging into the soft ground and throwing up fountains of black mould as it plunged ahead, leaving Shingas in its wake. With the horse moving at full gallop through the trees, Esther stole a look over her shoulder and saw that Shingas was falling behind. Looking back a few moments later he was lost from sight altogether.

With day and night colliding, the horse burst out from the trees onto a sandy slip of land. Instantly Esther pulled back on the rein, turning its head and bringing to a stop at the edge of the lake which lay before them, its shimmering surface turned to liquid gold by the rays of the setting sun. Taking a moment to survey the wide expanse of water with its palisade of towering trees, Esther knew they were trapped. Then her mind made up, without a moment's hesitation Esther spurred the horse forward into the lake, splashing through the shallows until the water deepened. Instinctively, thrashing out with its legs the horse began to swim and as it moved out into the lake Esther slid off its back and lowering herself into the icy water, she pushed the French girl forward until she was able to grab hold of the horse's mane. Looking up at her with the same reassuring smile on her face, Esther kicked out with her legs and pulling her arms through the water she began swimming alongside the horse, every stroke taking her further out into the lake. Behind them the shoreline faded away. Ahead, the dark outline of the trees beckoned to them with the promise of sanctuary.

As the golden orb of the dying sun sank beneath the horizon at the western end of the lake, Esther began to feel the icy chill of the water eating into her very bones. Her arms and legs were becoming leaden. The sodden doeskin dress weighing her down like a suit of chain-mail, her head at times disappearing completely beneath the rippling wavelets. In desperation she pulled the strap of the satchel over her head and let it slip from her fingers, watching as the carry-all, filled with food she had secretly squirrelled away for just such an opportunity, disappeared beneath the murky waters. Even free of this burden, slowly, inexorably fatigue began to take its toll and Esther began falling behind. Seeing her struggling to keep up, the French girl, her hands knotted in the mane of the horse stared down at her, anxiety and fear etched onto her small face, her eyes like saucers. Esther responded by redoubling her efforts but her strength was quickly ebbing away and she began to flounder. Horrified, the girl cried out to her, words which she could not understand but whose meanings were clear. Seeing the horse pulling ahead of her, in one last despairing effort, Esther reached out and grabbed the animal's tail, clinging on desperately and crying with joy when she felt herself being dragged along in its wake.

Standing on the narrow beach Shingas gazed out across the broad expanse of water, witnessing Esther's audacity with a sense of admiration. Eventually losing sight of them in the fading light he turned his back on the lake and moved away into the surrounding trees. The white woman's bravery had saved her for now but for Shingas it was not over.

When the horse's hooves touched the bank on the far shore, with one final effort the exhausted animal plunged forward out of the lake dragging Esther behind it like a landed fish. Done in, it stood head down, nostrils flared, its tired legs trembling uncontrollably. Elated, the French girl slid down from its back and dashed across to where Esther lay sprawled on the beach the water lapping at her feet.

Falling onto her knees beside her, the girl threw her arms around Esther neck, tears of happiness running down her cheeks. Esther smiled up at her through the strands of hair plastered to her face, a smile of relief that they were both safe. Then slowly pulling herself up onto her feet she walked unsteadily across to the horse. Running her hands lovingly across its coat, still slick with water, Esther wrapped her arms around its broad neck and pressing her face into its matted mane, she whispered over and over in a hushed voice.

'Thank you. Thank you. Thank you.'

Shivering with cold Esther and the girl then stripped off their dresses, putting them on again once they had wrung them out as best they could. With their supper lying at the bottom of the lake, and night closing in, Esther made up a bed under one of the trees, and huddling together for warmth the pair were soon asleep.

As the morning sun climbed into the sky, narrow shafts of sunlight pierced the canopy of branches and fell like a spotlight on Esther and the French girl asleep like spoons, together on a bed of leaves. Warmed by the touch of sunlight, Esther woke with a start and instantly looked around her. Panic-stricken she scrambled to her feet. The horse was gone.

Rushing out from the encircling trees Esther spotted the horse grazing on a narrow grassy strand between the lake and the forest and filled with relief she walked towards it. As she drew near the horse lifted its head and laying back its ears it moved away from her. Esther stopped, waited a moment and then walked toward it again, holding out her hand and speaking softly to it. Skittish, the horse pawed at the ground with its hoof and moved farther away. Terrified that it might gallop off, Esther stopped and stood watching as it began feeding on the grass once more. Uncertain as to how she might resolve this impasse, Esther was horrified when she saw the French girl walk out from the trees and approach the horse speaking to it as she did so in a soft but firm voice.

'Mauvais cheval! Mauvais cheval! Toujours tu avez faim. Tu etes un mauvais cheval.'[1]

Instantly the horse lifted its head and pricked up its ears. Terrified that the animal would take fright and run off, Esther looked on with amazement as it simply stood motionless and allowed the girl to walk up to it. Gently stroking the horse's nose, the French girl took hold of the makeshift rein and beaming with delight, she led the young mare over to where Esther stood, relief etched onto her face.

After breakfasting on blueberries and a shared handful of wild strawberries, Esther and the French girl mounted the horse and after taking her bearings from the sun, Esther kicked the horse into motion. In moments they were moving at a canter through the deep woods. The trees were more spaced now and

---

[1]   Bad horse! Bad horse! Always you are hungry. You are a bad horse.

keeping the sun on her right shoulder, Esther urged the young mare on, anxious that Shingas might still be following them. Up ahead a narrow defile funnelled them towards a stand of ancient hemlocks, their massive trunks and sturdy branches worth their weight in gold to any shipbuilder. Cast into shadow by the dense canopy of leaves, suddenly without warning, whinnying with fright the horse reared up, throwing Esther and the girl from its back and onto the ground. Confronting the frightened animal, Shingas calmly raised his musket, aimed at its head and fired. The explosion reverberated through the woods and mortally wounded the horse went down, its legs trying one last run and then it lay still, its life snuffed out by an ounce of lead. Clutching the whimpering girl tightly to her, Esther watched as Shingas strode towards them, as always his features giving no clue as to his intentions. Standing over them Shingas stared down menacingly. Esther stared back at him, sensing a look of indecision in his gaze, it was almost as though he was unsure of what he should do. But then the moment was gone and without a word or gesture, Shingas turned his back on them and walked away through the stand of giant trees. Nonplussed Esther stared after him, then realising why he had abandoned them, she took hold of the French girl's hand and hurried after him before he was swallowed up by the forest.

With night approaching Shingas reached his village and with Esther and the French girl following a few paces behind him, the girl clinging tightly to Esther's hand, he made his way towards its centre. When they reached the quadrangle Esther saw that a large crowd, men, women and children had gathered, closing around them in a large circle. Immediately, Shingas stepped aside and moving away, he disappeared into the encircling crowd, leaving Esther and the girl standing alone at its centre, a focus for the sea of condemning eyes surrounding them. Esther cast her own eyes over the watching crowd looking for the old squaw, hoping that if she saw them she may offer them some hope, but all she saw was a squaw pushing and elbowing her way through the crowd. Watching her as she broke free from the throng of people, Esther glimpsed the locket hanging around her neck and instantly she knew who she was. With a look of triumph on her hard face, Tekakwitha strutted up to Esther and taking hold of the French girl's hand, she wrenched her free. Powerless to intervene, shame-faced, Esther watched as, screaming and struggling, she led the girl away dropping her head as accompanied by a loud chorus of approval from the savage audience, the pair disappeared into the crowd.

Moments later a hush descended on the crowd and raising her head Esther watched with dismay as a large group of squaws, each carrying a stout stick or club, walked forward and silently, ominously, formed up facing each other in two long lines. One of them she recognised instantly, her beautiful face contorted into a look of pure hatred. Meeataho was not going to miss this opportunity. Realised now that this was to be her punishment and remembering what she had seen on her way to the stream that day, Esther spun around, frantically searching the crowd for Shingas but he was nowhere to be seen. Resigned, Esther steeled herself and suddenly wanting desperately to get it over with, she drew a deep breath and rushed headlong into the space between the two rows of squaws. A great shout went up and the crowd surged forward clamouring for a better view. Running as fast as her weary legs would carry her, with an arm raised protectively in front of her face, Esther plunged ahead.

Shrieking like demons the waiting squaws struck out at her with their sticks and clubs. A vicious blow from one dropped her to her knees but instinctively she climbed to her feet and staggered blindly forward. Seizing her chance Meeataho thrust out her leg and sent Esther sprawling onto the ground. In a flash Meeataho was standing over her, her face convulsed with fury and with Esther lying helpless at her feet, she raised her club high above her head and began raining blow after blow down on her, beating her mercilessly. Racked with pain Esther wanted to cry out but she was determined not to show any weakness. Suddenly Shingas was there and as Meeataho raised her club once more, he grabbed a handful of the young squaw's hair. Dragging her away, he snatched the club from her hand and threw her to the ground. Like a caged animal Meeataho glared up at him, defiant. Shingas fixed her with a deadly stare and said something to her, his voice imbued with menace. Shocked by his words, Meeataho backed away and with a last hate filled stare she got up off her knees, turned and stormed away.

Throwing aside the club, Shingas turned to Esther, sprawled out at his feet, blood running freely down her face from a deep cut in her forehead. Before he can say or do anything the old squaw appeared out of nowhere and hovering over Esther she fixed Shingas with her eyes. This was the moment. Staring back at her, Shingas gave an imperceptible nod then turned and strode away. Smiling in triumph through her blackened teeth, the old squaw took hold of Esther's arm and helped her to her feet, then supporting her with an arm about her waist, she walked Esther back to their long-house. When they reached the doorway Esther suddenly stopped and reaching out she gripped the door-post while at the same time, with her other hand pressed against her stomach, she began retching. With a knowing smile on her wrinkled face the old squaw looked on. When Esther had fled, her world had been plunged into darkness but now the Yenge woman had been returned to her and more than that, she carried her son's child in her belly.

CHAPTER NINE

E STHER STOOD OVER the cooking-fire slowly stirring the contents of the pot suspended over it, her other hand resting on her distended stomach. The realisation that she was pregnant had struck her hard at first but from being unwanted, as the infant grew within her womb, so too did her longing for it to be born. Even before she herself had been totally sure, word of her condition had spread like wild-fire among the squaws and instantly their animosity towards her had melted away and everywhere she was greeted by smiles and gestures of kindness. Even Takakwaitha's frosty heart had thawed a little and much to their delight, the French girl was allowed to visit with her from time to time. With her sunburned face and wearing a doeskin dress and moccasins the French girl was now indistinguishable from the other children and when, sitting patiently with only the occasional wriggle, she had allowed Esther to plat her hair into a braid, the transformation was complete.

During the long winter with the forest buried deep in snow and the trees cracking like muskets in the bitter cold, the long evenings of midwinter had been a wonderful time for both Esther and the child. Snug in the warmth of the long-house they would cluster around the lodge-fire with other families, warriors, squaws and children, laughing and jesting, with the pipe passing around from hand to hand. Being a part of these convivial gatherings, Esther witnessed a gentler, more endearing side to these savage people and she took enjoyment from it. Occasionally, a wizened old warrior, one of the villages story-tellers, the firelight playing across his ancient face, would enthral the gathering with stories of long dead spirits and monsters, striking fear into his superstitious audience with tales of witches and vampires. Although unable to understand what he was saying, Esther and the girl still found themselves as enthralled as the all-believing souls crowded around them, feasting on his words.

Even at such joyful times as these Shingas would rarely make an appearance and when he did, he would sit apart, silent and brooding, taking no part in the merrymaking. Once, unaware Esther had caught him looking at her swollen belly and felt from his gaze that he took pleasure from her condition but that his stoicism would not let it show on his face. Given his long periods of absence since the night that he had ravished her, she had sometimes wondered if perhaps it was a feeling of remorse that kept him from sharing a bed with her instead of leaving her free to have the child in her cot. Then she would push the thought from her mind, after all how could someone like her be able to fathom the depths of such a savage heart. No it was more likely she convinced herself, that he would be lying with the squaw Meeataho. If this were true, it had made little difference to their relationship, for whenever Esther had offered her a friendly smile, the young squaw would simply scowl back at her and look away.

Despite such displeasing thoughts Esther took great pleasure from these evenings and much to her delight on one of them, quite unexpectedly the girl had turned to her and pointing a finger at herself, she had told her that her name was Chantal. Touched by the child's innocent revelation, Esther had responded by placing a finger on her own chest and revealing her own identity.

Smiling with joy the two had then embraced, truly bound together now, as close to each other as if they had been born as sisters and in that moment Esther vowed that she would care for this orphaned waif as though she were her own flesh and blood.

Appearing in the doorway of the long-house, Chantal called to Esther her voice filled with excitement.

'Esther venez vite, venez vite.'

Slowly Esther turned towards her. During the long winter months they had both endeavoured to learn the language of their captors. With her nimble brain the child had found it quite easy and soon spoke it as fluently as any Seneca child. But for Esther the task had proved too much and she quickly gave it up as hopeless. As a compromise, they decided that they would each teach the other a few basic words in their own language and while this was successful to a degree, for the most part they got by with facial expressions and gestures. Frustrated by Esther's lack of urgency, Chantal called out again, remembering this time to use the English words she had been taught.

'Come, quick. Come quick.'

Smiling at the girl's impatience, Esther lifted the pot off the fire and walked towards the doorway.

Hand in hand, with Chantal pulling on Esther's arm in the hope that she would walk a little faster, the pair made their way through the village, quickly finding themselves engulfed in a noisy crowd of people, all making their way towards the quadrangle. Reaching the centre of the village and still clutching each other's hand, they wove their way through the gathering throng until they reached the inner ring of spectators. Unaware of the reason for this sudden urgent migration to the quadrangle, Esther was shocked to see Shingas standing at its centre with a dozen warriors armed with muskets grouped around him, their faces painted for war. She had not seen him for several days and as she stared at his cruel features, emblazoned with war-paint, her heart shuddered with dread.

Sensing that the moment was right, Shingas raised his arms aloft and instantly a hush descended over the watching crowd. Off to one side, huddled together in a tight group, Wapontak and a handful of elders looked on with hooded eyes, helpless spectators to the events that were about to unfold. Sweeping his gaze over the sea of faces, Shingas suddenly strode across to where a warrior stood a little way apart from the others with a blanket around his shoulders. Reaching out a hand, Shingas seized a corner of the blanket and with a wild shout, pulled it off him, revealing the warrior's back. Gasps of horror rose up from the crowd when they saw the marks left by the whip, the exposed flesh a lattice-work of bloody stripes, deep and raw. Savouring the moment, Shingas thrust the blanket into the warrior's outstretch hand and turning to face his savage audience he began to speak, his voice loud and impassioned, his finger pointing towards the warrior who had received the whipping.

'This is how the English treat the warriors of the Onondowaga.' He paused, letting his words sink in. 'Their redcoat soldiers have defeated our French brothers and now while their Great Father sleeps, they walk with a broad and heavy foot upon our land and treat us like dogs.'

An angry murmuring rippled through the crowd, his words striking a chord in many of their hearts.

'These English are not like our French brothers, they do not wish to be our friends, their only desire is to steal our lands away from us and to drive us into the wilderness.' And then in a rising voice. 'I say it is time to take up the hatchet my people and drive these English from our land before we too are swallowed up by them.'

With their thirst for blood and vengeance aroused, the crowd roared their approval and whipped into a frenzy of hatred, the warriors among them surged forward, their war-cries resounding into the forest. Pressed in on all sides by the crowd Esther suddenly clutched her stomach, her face contorted with pain. Her contractions had started.

Constructed as the name would suggest, by the French, Fort Le Boeuf was built to guard the southern end of the portage between French Creek and Lake Eire some fifteen miles upstream. Standing on high ground overlooking the Venango River, a tributary of the Allagheny, with the defeat of the French in 1759 the British had taken possession of the fort and it was now garrisoned by an Ensign, two corporals and eleven privates. Surrounded by a low palisade wall of logs driven upright into the ground and standing twelve feet above it, each sharpened at the top and some set with a loop-hole from which small-arms could be fired. Entry to the fort was gained through a single gate with a bastion on either side from where, after climbing a ladder, a sentry could look out along the track leading away towards the surrounding forest, or gaze out upon the slowly flowing river below.

Inside the palisaded square, a small guard-house and log barracks with a bark roof ran the length one wall. Set into a corner, with two of its walls forming a corner of the stockade, was an impressive, two storey windowless blockhouse constructed of logs caulked with mud and set upon stone foundations. Fluttering proudly from the flagpole above its shingle roof was the flag of St George.

It was one of the corporals who saw them first. Looking to supplement their meagre evening meal of boiled meat and corn, he had spent his off-duty time down at the river and was now returning with a fine catch of bass and perch. Looking up he witnessed, first in disbelief and then in horror a mass of armed Seneca warriors, their faces daubed with war-paint, emerging from the encircling trees and racing towards the fort. Cursing the idle sentry under his breath, he dropped his rod and catch and running for all he was worth, he sprinted towards the open gates of the fort, screaming out a warning as he ran towards them.

Hearing the corporal's cry, the sentry popped his head above the bastion and seeing the attacking Indians racing along the track towards the fort, he instinctively raised his musket and fired a bullet into them. Watching with satisfaction as a leading warrior froze in mid stride and then fell to the ground like a puppet whose wires had suddenly been cut in two. Below him the corporal had reached the gates and was frantically trying to push them shut. Without bothering to reload, the sentry crossed to the ladder and clambered down it to the ground. Behind him, the door to the barracks opened and seven soldiers, alerted by the musket fire and each clutching their flint-lock musket, spilled out, concern etched on their faces. Seeing them the corporal called out, shouting out to them in a loud voice, while desperately trying to close the open gate.

'Over here! Quickly, we must close the gate before.'

The words died in his throat as with a savage yell a Seneca warrior slashed at him with his hatchet, the blade slicing across the soldier's neck, and almost decapitating him. A spume of blood bubbling up from the gaping hole in the dying man's windpipe.

With Shingas at their head and shrieking their war-cries the horde of Indians poured in through the half-closed gate. Suddenly finding himself engulfed by the onrushing Indians, the sentry lashed out with the butt of his musket, desperately trying to defend himself. Seizing his chance, Cattawa pushed the muzzle of his musket into the soldier's chest and pulled the trigger, crying out as the lead ball tore through cloth and flesh until it reached the soldier's heart, killing him instantly. Witnessing the death of their comrades and realising the futility of attempting to close the gates, the seven soldiers fired a ragged volley into the

Indians and slowly retreated towards the blockhouse. Screaming with hatred when they saw several of their number hit by the hail of bullets, the Seneca returned fire, whooping as three of the soldiers collapsed onto the ground, blood oozing from their wounds. Suddenly the door to the blockhouse was flung open and appearing in the doorway, the Ensign screamed out to the beleaguered survivors.

'In here! In here!'

Without needing further encouragement and with their blood-thirsty enemy thankfully busy with their scalping knives, the survivors seized on the chance and backed away towards the open blockhouse door. Spotting them, Shingas yelled out above the din and instantly a dozen warriors raised their muskets and poured a volley into them. Miraculously, two of the four survived the hail of bullets and reached the open doorway. Dragging them inside, the Ensign slammed the heavy door shut. Outside, the groans of the wounded were quickly silenced by war-clubs and the tomahawk.

With their enemy trapped inside the blockhouse, Pahotan and a group of warriors, armed with muskets, ran across to the soldiers' barracks. Slipping inside, they knocked away several planks in the wall with the butts of their rifles and opened fire on the blockhouse, aiming for the loop-holes set at intervals in the two walls, which faced into the fort.

Crouched down beside the half open gate, the body of the dead corporal sprawled at his feet, Shingas looked across at the blockhouse. Seeing what must be done, he signalled to a group of warriors armed with bows and quivers of arrows. Gathering them around him he spoke urgently to one of them, and immediately warrior turned away and ran towards the barracks. As soon as he had gone, Shingas pulled out his knife and reaching down he slashed open the front of the dead soldiers tunic and began cutting away part of his shirt. Tearing it into strips, he handed them to the watching warriors. Inside the barracks, the warrior found the small store room at the far end and forcing open the door he scoured the crowded shelves. Finding what he had been told to look for he took down the small keg of tar oil and clutching it to him like a prized possession, he ran from the building.

With a single blow of his hatchet, Shingas removed the lid from the keg and one by one the group of bowmen dipped an arrow, with a strip of the corporal's shirt wrapped around the end of its shaft, into the oil. Snatching a flaming torch from one of the warriors, Shingas set light to the saturated cloth, watching as the archers raise their bows and shot their fiery missiles into the air. In the encroaching darkness the arrows rained down like blazing comets onto the blockhouse's shingle roof, the glow from their flames growing brighter as they took hold.

Inside, the blockhouse comprised of a single square shaped room with rows of loopholes set into each wall. The lower ones at the height of a man's shoulder, the upper ones reached by climbing a ladder up to a narrow gallery landing. Illuminated by a pair of lanterns hanging from hooks in the wall, four soldiers stood at their stations firing through the loopholes. The crash of their muskets was deafening and the acrid smoke from their discharge hung in the air like a cloud. Standing beside a makeshift table, its rough planks cleared of everything except for ramrods, an open keg of gunpowder, musket balls scattered like marbles and thin strips of wadding, a fifth soldier and the young Ensign worked methodically, each reloading muskets and thrusting them into the eager hands of their comrades at the loopholes in exchange for the one they had just fired. From time to time the young Ensign cast an anxious look up at the roof, watching as the corporal, after filling a bucket from the well in the corner, climbed again and again to the gallery above and threw the contents onto the burning timbers above.

Sensing a slackening of the fire from outside, one of the soldiers lent forward and peered out through his loophole. Instantly a hail of musket balls pattered like hailstones against the blockhouse wall and pitching backwards he fell mortally wounded onto the floor, a bloody hole where his right eye had once been. Staring down at the dead soldier, the loader quickly armed himself with a musket and took his place at the loophole, brushing at his hair as burning embers rained down from the inferno above. With little hope of extinguishing the flames, the corporal had thrown the bucket down and wielding an axe, he worked desperately to enlarge the hole he had managed to hack out in the rear wall. Behind him a soldier screamed out and staggered back from his loophole clutching his face. Reaching out the young Ensign took him into his arms, gently lowering the dying man to the floor. As he did so, above him, devoured by the voracious flames the roof beams finally gave way, sending the blazing roof collapsing down on them.

Outside, whooping and howling like devils possessed the Seneca warriors watched as the roof caved in. With exultant cries, several of them ran up to the blockhouse walls and fired their muskets into it through the empty loopholes. As they did so the blockhouse door was suddenly flung open and the young ensign appeared, framed in the doorway his hair and clothing ablaze. Shrieking in agony he ran into the stockade, a human torch, his piercing screams rending the night. Crowding around the pitiable figure screaming in delight at his agony, the crowd of warriors looked on as his skin melted like butter in the conflagration. Finally, unable to endure the torture any longer, the wretched soul fell to his knees and curling into the foetal position, he surrendered his body to the all-consuming flames.

SHINGAS

Outside the stockade, unseen and unnoticed, the corporal emerged from the enlarged hole he had made in the blockhouse wall and like a nocturnal badger he set off at a stumbling run towards the welcoming darkness of the forest. Behind him the sky was lurid with flames, the air filled with the savage cries of the victors.

Inside the long-house illuminated by flaming torches Esther squatted on a blanket gripping tightly onto two wooden posts driven into the ground at each side of her. She was naked and her body glistened with perspiration. Suddenly she cried out as another contraction gripped her body and the urge to push down became almost unbearable. Kneeling at her side, the old squaw shook her head, and leaning forward she offered Esther a short stick to bite on. Esther turned her head away. Getting slowly to her feet the old squaw crossed to where a large pot hung suspended over the fire and dipping her hand into the simmering water she removed a piece of doeskin. Ringing off the excess water, she returned to Esther and gently ran the cloth over her face and neck, wiping away the sweat from her brow and pushing the lank strands of hair from her eyes.

Dropping her chin onto her chest, desperate to lie down, Esther was once again gripped by the urge to push. Staring despairingly at the old squaw she was overjoyed to see her nodding her head vigorously and encouraging her to push. Bearing down with all her strength, with one final scream, consumed by an exquisite pain Esther felt the child slip from her. Drained, Esther threw back her head and releasing her grip on the two bearing posts she slumped back against the wall, totally exhausted. With a joyful shout the old squaw scooped up the infant in her hands, cradling it in her arms until it gave its first lusty cry, then satisfied that all was as it should be, she handed Esther her new-born child.

'Be proud you have a fine son.'

Smiling, Esther took the baby from her and held him to her swollen breast. From the moment she knew for certain that she was pregnant, she had prayed that she would give birth to a boy. Now here he was, soft and warm against her skin, his tiny eyes screwed tightly shut, his shock of black hair plastered against his head. She knew that they would give him his name and that he would be called by it always, they were after all his people. But to her he would be Daniel and when she dared, she would whisper it to him while he slept. It had been her dead brother's name, he had lived four days longer than her mother who after three days on her bearing-stool had died giving him life. Long enough for him to be baptised and to be loved and hated in equal measure for all his short life. Although it had no influence on her choice, she also thought it a was fitting name for one born into such a lion's den as her son had surely been.

Half-running, half-staggering the corporal moved through the towering trees. Last night under cover of darkness he had got as far away from the fort as he dare without losing his way and then lain low at the edge of a cedar swamp, hardly daring to close his eyes. At dawn he had set out again, skirting the boggy ground and moving south towards the river knowing that with God's good grace it would lead him to Fort Pitt and safety. By mid-morning, and with the hills climbing before him, he laboured up a steep wooded incline. Reaching a vantage point, he was overjoyed to see below him, glimpsed through a break in the trees, a silver horseshoe of water, the Alleghany River, its slow flowing waters his road to salvation. Later that same afternoon his heart sank when climbing a high ridge he saw to the west, in the direction of Fort Venango, a plume of black smoke rising above the trees and immediately he knew that the fort had suffered the same fate as his own post. Filled with despair he plunged back into the forest, the will to survive driving him on.

Sweltering in the heat of the day the two sentries lounged outside the gates of the fort, cursing their luck and the NCO who had drawn up the duty roster. Suddenly their reverie was broken by the sound of the soldier stationed in the bastion above the gates shouting down to them.

'Look to!' And pointing with his outstretched arm. 'There down the road.'

Alerted, the two sentries swung around and staring down the road they saw the figure of a man staggering towards them. In an instant, setting their muskets aside, they raced towards him. Overwhelmed with relief at the sight of the gates and the two soldiers running towards him, the corporal, half dead from hunger and exhaustion dropped onto his knees. Barely conscious, when the two soldiers reached him, he gazed up at them bleary eyed, muttering his gratitude through blistered lips. Slipping an arm under each of his, supporting him between them, the two sentries half carried, half dragged the corporal through the gates and inside the walls of the fort.

Revived by two fingers of fine French brandy and heartened by the promise of a meal of stewed meat and potatoes to come, the corporal, escorted by one of the sentries, was led up a flight of stairs and into a spacious airy room dominated by a large mahogany desk. Seated at the desk, with letters and books scattered across its faded leather surface was the fort's commander Captain Simeon Ecuyer. A broad shouldered man with a thick neck, his austere features were overshadowed by a strong chin, jutting out like the prow of a ship. Of Swiss nationality, like many of his fellow countrymen he had been commissioned into service with the British army during the war with the French by no lesser personage than the Duke of Cumberland, such was the high regard afforded them as professional soldiers.

Seeing the corporal standing before him on unsteady legs, too weary even to throw up a salute, Captain Ecuyer barked at the sentry. 'Fetch a chair for this fellow, has he not endured enough?'

Chafing at the officers words, the sentry shouldered his musket and crossing the room he took hold of one of the heavy wooden chairs set on either side of the narrow window and carried it across to where the corporal stood. With a grateful nod the exhausted NCO slumped into it, glad to be off his feet. Waiting until the corporal had settled himself, Captain Ecuyer fixed him with a steady gaze and asked in a more reasonable voice.

'Is it true what I am told, that Fort Le Boeuf is destroyed?'

'Aye sir and Venango too. Both gone.'

At hearing the news confirmed, the officer slumped back in his chair, then composing himself he said.

'Venango also! Good God. Can you be sure?'

'Sure as what I saw with my own two eyes. T'was nothing else could cause such smoke as I seen and coming from where I knew the fort to be.'

Captain Ecuyer stared down at his hands, clenching them into fists until the knuckles where white.

'And it was Mingos who did this, who attacked you?'

'Aye, Seneca they was. They came on us without warning, a hundred of the murdering devils, maybe more.'

'And no others survived save yourself?'

Meeting the officer's steady gaze, when the corporal replied his words were imbued with sadness.

'None. Most died a'fore they made the blockhouse. The last ones I seen alive was Ensign Price and young Grey and they perished in the fire poor souls. I tried to save them, Lord knows I tried but the flames they was too fierce.'

Feeling the man's pain Captain Ecuyer softened his expression and leaning forward over his desk he replied.

'Don't reproach yourself, none here doubts your bravery, you have shown as much in bringing us your terrible news.' Then turning his head towards the door be bellowed out. 'Orderly! Orderly!'

Immediately the door opened and a youthful, smartly dressed soldier stepped into the room.

Addressing the orderly, Captain Ecuyer pointed towards the corporal.

'See to it that this brave fellow is given a hearty meal and a tot or two of rum to wash it down.'

With an impudent grin the orderly replied.

'There are many who say he should be given the whole barrel sir.'

Allowing himself a half smiling Captain Ecuyer replied, a slightly derisory tone to his voice.

'Indeed he does but I fear a drunken corporal with a head as sore as a Quaker's knee, would be a poor reward for their generosity.'

Suitably reprimanded, the orderly quickly crossed the room and helping the corporal to his feet, he led him out of the room, closing the heavy wooden door behind them. Gathering his thoughts, Captain Ecuyer reached out a hand and picking up his pen he said to the sentry.

'Find the Sergeant at arms and have him send me an express-rider. Oh, and say that he is to saddle my bay gelding.'

Sensing the need for urgency, the sentry turned about and hurried from the room. Behind him Captain Ecuyer dipped his quill into the inkwell and with scratchy strokes of the pen he began writing his despatch.

With no more than thirty minutes having passed since the corporal was escorted into the safety of the fort, the gates swung open again and mounted on the big bay gelding, its burnished coat gleaming in the bright sunlight, the express-rider rode out. Cheered on by the watching sentries he racing away down the stretch of dirt road, reins flapping, the horse's hooves kicking up clouds of dust as it broke into a gallop.

The Forbes Road as it was called, had been completed in 1758 during the war with the French. Built by the sweated labour of troops under the command of Brigadier General Forbes, when finished it ran for three hundred miles through the wilderness, from Fort Pitt in the west, to the township of Carlisle in the eastern settlements.

Constructed so that troops and supplies could be more easily transported to the isolated outposts along its torturous route, in truth it was little more than a track hacked through the forest. Snaking its way over hills and gullies and hemmed in for most of its length by towering trees and narrow defiles. To express-riders however, given that it meant at least two days less in the saddle, the road was as welcome as a woman's warm body on a cold winter's night.

After two hours hard riding the express-rider spotted a column of black smoke rising above the trees not a quarter mile from the road. Fearing and doubting in equal measure, cursing aloud, he pulled on the reigns and turning off the road onto what was at best a rutted track, he kicked the horse towards the offending cloud.

At full gallop he swept into the patch of cleared ground with a small cabin at its centre and saw with some relief that the smoke he had seen was not the work of the savages but came instead from a bonfire of uprooted tree stumps. Pulling on the reigns he brought the horse to a halt and swinging around in the saddle he stared across to where a homesteader was straining on a stout pole the end of which was tightly wedged beneath the roots of an exposed stump. Opposite him a horse, harnessed to the stump by chains and rope, was being led away by a young lad with skinny legs and a freckled face. Off to the side, a growing pile of tree stumps bore witness to their labours. As the rope tightened, distracted by the express-rider's sudden appearance, the man shouted out something to the boy and relaxing his hold on the pole he turned to face the horseman who had interrupted their work. Catching his breath the express-rider called out to them.

'The Indians have taken up the hatchet, best you take your family and go into the fort.'

Even as he spoke, the man's wife, a mousy haired woman in her early twenties and dressed in a simple linen frock, buttoned at the neck and cuffs, ran out from the cabin. Clutching tightly to her hand was a young girl no more than five wearing a long gingham dress, her milky white face framed by ringlets of golden curls growing half-way to her waist. The woman had caught his words and with her pretty face clouded with uncertainty, she called out.

'Are we not safe here? We have done them no harm.'

Pulling back on the reigns the express-rider turned his horse around until he faced the anxious woman.

'That's as maybe but you must go into the fort. You'll be safe there. Hurry now the Indians will be here soon.'

Behind him the man gave an indifferent shrug of the shoulders and turning away he gave his attention once more to the tree stump. Seeing the look of concern on the woman's face the express-rider leaned forward in his saddle and called out to her.

'Go to Fort Pitt. Hurry now and all will be well.'

Then kicking his heels into his mount, he raced away, the horse's hooves drumming on the sun baked ground. With her heart racing the woman hurried across to her husband and fighting to keep the fear from her voice she said.

'Should we not heed his warning?'

Pushing the pole under the half buried stump her husband glanced towards her and replied in a condescending voice.

'Don't fret so wife, we're as safe here as in any fort.'

Unimpressed by his casual assurance she spoke again, her voice infected with concern.

'But you heard his warning, should we not do as he said?'

Throwing aside the pole the husband turned on her angrily, a hard edge to his voice.

'What abandon our home and trudge fifteen miles on the say so of some express-rider.' Then with a note of finality in his voice. 'No, best we stay here. All will be well, you'll see.'

After a gruelling two day ride, and having only stopped for a few hours at Fort Bedford to take some refreshment and to rest his brave horse, at dawn the express-rider was back in the saddle, the urgency of his mission driving him on. The officer at the fort had offered him a fresh mount but he had refused. He knew there was no better animal to have under him than Captain Ecuyer's Cleveland Bay and he was determined that together they should see this thing done.

With the wilderness behind them and with fewer trees to shade them from the heat of the July sun, the exhausted express-rider pulled off the road. Finding a shady spot with a stream nearby, he unsaddled the bay and after letting it drink a little, he tethered it to a tree. Wanting desperately to remove his boots but knowing full well that if he did he'd not get them on again, the express-rider contented himself by unbuttoning his jacket and after a meal of cold cuts of meat and dry biscuits, he stretched out full length on the rough ground and fell into a sound sleep.

Having slept longer than he had intended and with nightfall approaching, the express-rider fed his mount the last of the oats and with a bright moon to guide them he climbed back into the saddle and kicking the horse into a run set off into the night. Keeping to a steady canter, the miles slipped by and as the first golden rays of sunlight pierced the dawn sky they came at last to a sentry post on the outskirts of Philadelphia manned by a bleary eyed soldier. Reigning in his mount the express-rider called out to him for directions.

After a thankless night of guarding the good folk of Philadelphia, all safely tucked up in their feather beds and feeling the morning chill creeping into his bones, the sentry was not in the best of moods. Even the sustaining thoughts of the hearty breakfast and welcome bed which awaited him were waning. So while the sudden arrival of the express-rider relieved the tedium of his post, the rider's impatient shouts did little to improve his disposition. Swinging his musket across his chest and with his unfortunate face set in a belligerent scowl the sentry strode towards the horseman, calling out loudly as he approached him.

'Who goes there? State your business.'

Running a hand along the horse's neck, the express-rider replied as calmly as his growing mood of impatience allowed.

'I carry an urgent despatch for Colonel Bouquet.'

The sentry took a pace forward and stared up at the express-rider more determined than ever to be as unaccommodating as possible.

'And who might this despatch be from eh?'

Unable to restrain his anger the express-rider shouted back at him, his words laced with venom.

'What I carry and from whom are no concern of yours, now point me in the direction of the 60th Regiment of Foot.'

Stung by the rider's words yet finding himself quite enjoying the confrontation, the sentry replied with growing confidence.

'That may be so but you'll see nothing of the 60th till I'm told...'

Before he could finish the sentence, the words died in his throat as the express-rider spurred his horse forward and shouted threateningly.

'Damn you blockhead, I'll have those direction or so help me I'll ride over you and find the 60th myself.'

Shocked by the rider's words yet more worried at the prospect of being trampled under the horse hooves, the sentry backed away, muttering out loud.

'There's no need for threats, I have a duty.'

"Bugger your duty, I'll have those directions or the Colonel himself will hear of this and I doubt he'll treat you kindly, more likely a spell in the guardhouse is what you'll get for delaying his despatch.'

Realising that he had gone too far and knowing what was good for him, swallowing his indignation the sentry turned towards the distant town and pointed with his arm.

'Follow the road for a mile and where it forks take the road to the left, it's no more than a track but it will take you to the Headquarters of the 60th Regiment.'

Without bothering to give him the courtesy of a reply, the express-rider dug his heals into the horse's flanks and grinning as the sentry leapt clear of its flying hooves, he leaned forward over the bay's neck and with the molten orb of the sun rising above the roofs of the distant houses, he raced away.

Set in five acres of parkland and approached by a wide sweeping driveway lined by an avenue of towering beech trees,

Colonel Bouquet had chosen a fine imposing Georgian mansion from which to conduct his affairs.

Fronting the grand house was a large rectangular lawn, frequently used as a parade ground, with a tall flagpole set at its centre, the flag of St George fluttering from it in the warm morning breeze. Their drill completed, a company of redcoats marched away in two ranks, their bayonets gleaming in the early sunlight, their boots crunching on the road's gravelled surface. Striding along beside them, his chest pushed out, chin tucked in, their sergeant suddenly bellowed out an order and as though it were a well-rehearsed manoeuvre, the two files parted like the Red Sea allowing the express-rider to gallop between them. Closing ranks when he had passed and without breaking step, they continued along the road.

Reigning in his tired mount in front of the house, exhausted, the express-rider slid down from the saddle and stumbled towards its imposing double doors guarded by two sentries. Without issuing a challenge the nearest sentry seized hold of the gleaming brass handle and flung open the heavy door. It seemed the mail-pouch slung across his chest was all that was required to gain access. Once inside the cavernous hallway a Sergeant at Arms strode towards him across the marbled floor and blocked his path, his stern expression softening a little when he saw the fatigue etched into the express-rider's face.

'Well lad do you have news for us?'

'Aye sergeant I've an urgent despatch from Fort Pitt for Colonel Bouquet.'

Immediately the Sergeant at Arms crossed towards a pair of double doors set with inlaid panels and grasping both handles he pulled them open.

'In here lad.'

With the murmur of male voices spilling out into the hallway, the express-rider stepped gingerly into the room the doors closing behind him with barely a sound.

The room was not overly large with a high ceiling and polished floorboards. Devoid of colour, its walls were brightened by a number of ornately framed oil paintings depicting Constablesque landscapes. Its only furniture consisted of a large bow-fronted mahogany sideboard, festooned with fine silver plate and cut glass decanters. Standing in a group at its centre, glasses in hand, were a number of English officers, resplendent in their scarlet uniforms, the gold of their buttons gleaming in the sunlight which flooded in through the tall sash windows facing out onto the manicured lawn.

Becoming aware of the express-rider standing uncertainly in the doorway, the officers' strident conversations subsided into silence. Lowering his glass of port from his thin lips, a youthful looking lieutenant with a pallid complexion turned toward him and said in a reedy, humourless voice.

'Well man don't just stand there, state your business.'

Fumbling with the catch, the express-rider opened his mail-pouch and removed a document.

'If you please sir, I have an urgent dispatch from Fort Pitt for Colonel Bouquet.'

Instantly a path was cleared and Colonel Bouquet, a bright smile illuminating his face, emerged from the covey of officers and strode towards the express-rider. Of medium height and build with a rotund stomach, which strained energetically at the buttons of his waistcoat, there was little that was remarkable about him. Blessed with a full head of dark hair, his rounded face was set off by a long slender nose and a well-proportioned chin. Although these features and the cares of middle age combined to give him a scholarly appearance, the twinkle in his dark eyes hinted at a lighter side to his nature. When he spoke his voice betrayed a slight European accent, a testimony to his Swiss linage.

'Ah! News at last.'

Taking the despatch from the express-rider's proffered hand, Colonel Bouquet turned to one of the watching officers.

'Captain Bassett, be so kind as to instruct the Sergeant at Arms to take this brave fellow to the kitchen and to see that he is well fed and given a toddy to wash it down.' Then with a small smile playing across his face,

'I fear I may have need of him again before the day is out.'

With the express-rider at his heels Captain Bassett walked out through the doors. Behind them, Colonel Bouquet broke the wax seal and unfolded the despatch.

With his fears confirmed, within the hour the express-rider, well-nourished and furnished with a fresh mount, climbed back in the saddle and with his mail-pouch carrying a copy of Captain Ecyers despatch he set off at a gallop for New York. Also in his pouch was a letter from Colonel Bouquet giving support to Captain Ecyer's concerns and expressing in the gravest tones the need for urgent and immediate action by his Commander-in-chief. The importance of securing fort Pitt and the surrounding area against the savages he wrote was paramount. Little did he know that as the words dripped from his pen that war-parties were roaming the western frontier of Pennsylvania, attacking isolated settlements, killing their inhabitants, laying waste their homes and destroying the harvests.

Alone in his library with tome filled bookshelves lining all but one wall and at every window a heavy curtain drawn against the sunlight, Sir Jeffrey Amhurst, his asistocratic features marred somewhat by a down-turned mouth, paused in front of the Adam fireplace. In his late forties and wearing a plain but exquisitely tailored suit over a white shirt, ruffled at the neck and wrists he adjusted his spectacles, and continued reading the letter clutched in his hand.

The despatch from Fort Pitt with news of the loss of Fort Le Boeuf and Fort Venango, while pricking his conscience a little for persistently flattering himself that the uprising was an alarm that would soon subside, also brought forth a determination in him to stamp out this infamy and punish those villains responsible. So with his thoughts in order he crossed to the impressive desk which dominated the room and seating himself in a leather bound captain's chair, aided by the light from an ornate glass-bowled oil lamp he took up a quill pen and began writing a despatch to Colonel Bouquet.

> *Sir, Today I received your despatch with news of the loss of our posts at Venango and Le Boeuf and I intend to take every measure in my power to severely chastise those infamous villains who carried out this vile crime against His Majesty's subjects. To this end I have issued orders for Major Campbell to join you immediately with the light infantry companies of the seventeenth, forty second and seventy seventh Regiments. Thus reinforced you are to proceed with all speed to Fort Pitt and secure the garrison against the savages. Should any Indian tribes take up arms against you they are to be met with such force that is necessary to reduce them to reason. No punishment we can inflict is adequate to the vile crimes of these inhuman villains and I only need add that I do not wish to hear of any prisoners being taken. My orders are that should any*

savages who dare to take up arms against you, fall within your power, that they are to be put to death. Yours Sir Jeffrey Amhurst, Commander-in-Chief.

CHAPTER TEN

WITH THE END of July approaching and after a delay of some eighteen days while wagons and draught animals plus provisions for the campaign were collected, Colonel Bouquet and his little army of five hundred men finally broke camp and began their march. Riding at the head of the column with his officers, their horses' hooves kicking up clouds of dust into the morning air, Colonel Bouquet cast a look over his shoulder at his little force as it tramped along the street behind him. Watched by a crowd of silent onlookers, the sight of sixty invalid soldiers, unable to walk and being transported in open wagons did little to ease their anxiety. While not for one moment afraid of what lay ahead, Colonel Bouquet was nevertheless well aware that the task he had been entrusted with was not child's play.

Clear of the town, marching three abreast, the bare-legged Highlanders of the 42nd regiment in their kilts and plaids and the Grenadiers in their scarlet coats wound their way along the Cumberland valley. Behind them, lumbering over the bumpy track came the convoy of heavy wagons each drawn by a team of oxen and flanked by a guard of Light Infantry. Bringing up the rear were some two hundred pack-horses. Seperated into strings of twelve and managed by a pair of drivers hired for the task, every animal was heavily laden with supplies and sacks of flour.

On the fourth day after a gruelling trek along the badly neglected pioneer road, Colonel Bouquets little army, accompanied by the sound of the Grenadiers March played on fife and drum, marched into the frontier settlement of Bedford.

Hemmed in by the encircling mountains, the small township boasted a dozen or so log cabins each one surrounded by a strip of cultivated ground and the beginnings of an apple orchard. Dominating the small settlement was an impressive fort, named after the Duke of Bedford and giving its name to the scattering of dwellings clustered about it. Standing on raised ground above the west bank of the Juniata river, the fort's star shaped construction boasted a bastion at each of its five points with a deep ditch and a rampart of earth thrown up around it. The main gate faced to the south and as the fort was without a well, a wooden causeway with a planked roof had been constructed, which ran down to the river so that water could be fetched in relative safety.

Alerted by the music, families spilled out of their cabins, every soul filled with astonishment and joy at the sight of so many soldiers tramping down the dusty road towards them. At the fort the gates were swung open and hundreds of wretched fugitives who had fled their homes and sought sanctuary in the fort, spilled out and with clamorous shouts they quickly lined the road. From the ramparts above, the meagre garrison looked down with glad hearts and let out a rousing cheer.

With the joyful cries of his men ringing in his ears, Captain Lewis Ourry the fort's commanding officer, his portly figure threatening the constraints of a uniform at least one size too small, strode out through the gates and threw up his hand in a semblance of a salute.

Returning his salute, Colonel Bouquet dismounted and with a smile lighting up his face, he walked across to Captain Ourry and shook him by the hand. The two men were old friends, having been commissioned into the Royal American Regiment together in 1756 and where they had served together, Bouquet as the commanding officer of the first battalion and Ourry as his quartermaster. Ourry returned his colonel's smile and trying hard not to affect his voice with too much gratitude but without diminishing the warmth of his welcome he said.

'Your appearance as always sir is most timely and welcomed.'

With a contrived grimace Colonel Bouquet replied.

'And I sir have had enough of the saddle for one day.'

In Captain Ourry's quarters above the south bastion, Colonel Bouquet stepped back from the basin of hot water and taking the towel offered to him he began drying his face. Relieved of the towel, Ourry stepped over to a long oak table and picking up a crystal glass decanter he filled two glasses with generous amounts of port. Exchanging towel for glass, without a word, Colonel Bouquet walked over to the window and looked down into the fort. Although there was over an acre of open ground inside, it seemed that every inch was occupied with either a makeshift shelter housing a displaced family or his own oxen and wagons, all glad to be safe within its stout walls. Turning away, he put the glass to his lips and took a long swallow, savouring the warmth of the dark-red wine on his parched throat.

'So Lewis what news of Fort Pitt?'

Crossing to his desk, Captain Ourry removed a folded sheet of paper from a drawer and handed it to Colonel Bouquet, replying with a hard edge to his voice.

'This letter from Captain Ecuyer came by express three weeks ago... There has been no word since.'

Putting down his half-empty glass on the table, Colonel Bouquet opened the sheet of paper and began reading its contents, written in ink by a steady hand.

Fort Pitt July 16th

Sir, We have alarms from and skirmishes with the Indians every day; but they have done us little harm as yet. Yesterday I was out with a party of men when we were fired upon and one of the sergeants was killed; but we beat off the Indians and brought the man in with his scalp on. Last night the bullock guard was fired upon, when one of the cows was killed. We are obliged to be on duty night and day. The surrounding woods are full of prowling Indians whose number seem daily to increase; but we have plenty of provisions and the fort is in such a good posture of defence that with God's assistance, we can defend it against a thousand Indians. Yours Respectfully etcetera .. Simeon Ecuyer.

Folding the letter, Colonel Bouquet turned to face Captain Ourry.

'Three weeks ago you say?'

Captain Ourry nodded in confirmation.

'I pray we are in time.'

Before Captain Ourry could reply there was a loud knock at the door and a moment later it swung open and one of the garrison soldiers, his musket clutched in his hand stuck his head into the room.

'Beg pardon sir but the gentlemen you were expecting are here.'

Waiting until Colonel Bouquet had downed the last of his port and set the glass down on the table, Captain Ourry replied.

'Show them in lad.'

Pushing the door fully open the soldier quickly stood to attention and pulling his musket into his side, he called out in a robust voice.

'The captain will see you now.'

Immediately, three men strode into the room. All were middle aged or older and each was dressed in a coarse woollen jerkin and buckskin breeches. With a nod towards Captain Ourry, they fixed their eyes on Colonel Bouquet, their faces very serious. In exchange Colonel Bouquet gave them a warm smile but sensing from their posture and demeanour their reluctance to be here at all, he allowed it to dissolve and quickly got down to business.

'Thank you for coming Gentlemen.'

As though wishing to remind him of the hard task he faced, two of the men responded by folding their arms across their chests. Undeterred, Colonel Bouquet continued, his voice neither demanding nor condescending.

'I will speak frankly. I am ordered to proceed with all speed to Fort Pitt and to secure it against the Indians. In order to advance with greater speed I intend leaving behind a greater part of my oxen and wagons and to take such supplies as I can on pack-horses, which hopefully you can provide me with. Also given that my troops are no woodsmen and knowing the wild nature of the country and the opportunities it presents for ambush, I must seek to procure from amongst you as many woodsmen as possible to march with us.'

After exchanging glances, the spokesman for the three stepped forward and while his reply was not a refusal, his words carried little in the way of hope.

'We think Colonel that most men would prefer to remain here for the defence of their families.'

Knowing full well that there would be objections to his suggestion, Colonel Bouquet voiced his concession.

'I can well understand your concerns and for my part, I would be willing to leave additional troops at the fort for their protection.'

With a sneering look the man replied, mockery dripping from every word.

'Aye no doubt the ones so full of fight that you must transport them in wagons. What use are they to us pray tell me?'

Fighting back his anger at the man's assertion, and determined that the words he spoke and not the manner in which he said them should be enough of a rebuke to the man's insolence, Colonel Bouquet replied calmly.

'Don't judge those men too harshly or too readily sir. These brave fellows are no malingerers but are merely weakened by fever, a malaise contracted while fighting the King's enemies in Havana and I for one would happily entrust my own family's welfare to them, safe in the knowledge that I should not find them wanting.'

With his sneer replaced by a scowl, the spokesman dropped his head, turned and walked towards the door followed by his companions. As they filed out of the room, the last colonist to leave turned and spoke.

'You shall have your horses Colonel. I cannot say either way on the other matter except that I will speak in favour of it to any that will consider accompanying you.'

'I thank you sir. I shall march for Fort Pitt in two days from now.'

With a curt nod, the man left the room, closing the door shut behind him.

No sooner had the latch dropped when Captain Ourry blurted out.

'Damn their insolence.'

Smiling at Ourry's outburst Colonel Bouquet crossed to the table and picking up the decanter, he filled both glasses to the brim with the remains of the port. Taking care not to spill a drop, with a smile playing at the corner of his mouth, he handed one of the glasses to Captain Ourry.

'Oh I knew well they would be a hard nut to crack given their miserable suffering and knowing as they surely do, that Indian war-parties are still raiding all along the border, butchering men women and children.'

Knowing better than to pursue the subject further, Captain Ourry raised his glass and downing half the contents in a single swallow, he walked over to the window and gazing down on the hive of activity below he quickly changed tack.

'So Colonel I'm to be reinforced with your idle reprobates am I?'

With a feigned look of disapproval, the amused tone in Colonel Bouquet's voice spoke volumes for the friendship both men shared.

'Indeed you are sir, all sixty of them.'

'And for this I am to express my gratitude?'

'Come Lewis a day or two of fresh air and sunlight and their health will improve beyond measure.'

'You forget sir.' Ourry replied with a knowing look, 'that I am privy to the coarse nature of these fellows and well aware of the opportunities for debauchery afforded them in Manilla and all for the price of the King's shilling. So I doubt fresh air and sunlight alone will prove a cure for the disease that afflicts them.'

'That my good sir,' replied Colonel Bouquet, a measure of indignation in his tone of voice, 'is something you must speak about with someone more medically knowledgeable than I.' Concluding with a more serious note to his voice,

'I wished I could spare you more able bodied men but I fear I shall need all the troops at my disposal if I am to succeed in my task.'

Sensing that perhaps he had taxed the issue a little too much, Captain Ourry replied in a more contrite manner.

'Forgive my levity sir, I am of course most grateful for the additional troops and I only mock their condition out of sympathy for it.'

Draining the contents of his glass and sensing his subordinates discomfort Colonel Bouquet replied.

'Nonsense! A little light heartedness never goes amiss.' Then crossing towards the captains desk, 'but now I must trouble you for pen and paper Lewis, for I have a dispatch to write and an express to get away while there is still light enough for him to ride by.'

Even as the two officers spoke, two hundred miles away to the west, seated on her low cot, the infant fed and contented cradled in her arms, Esther watched with interest as the old squaw, her hands busy with an awl and a length of catgut began putting the finishing touches to a cradle board for her new grandson. In an instant, her attention was snatched away when, as if from nowhere Shingas stepped into the compartment, his savage features still emblazoned with war paint and a bloody scalp hanging from his belt.

Setting aside his musket, Shingas took in the scene of domesticity and then striding across to Esther he stared down at the baby. In a cackling voice the old squaw spoke up.

'You have a fine son.'

Unmoved by her words, Shingas remained silent his countenance seemingly carved out of wood. Apprehensive,

Esther looked up at him, becoming a little afraid. Suddenly Shingas reached out his hands. His voice demanding.

'Give me the child.'

Filled with dread, Esther drew back, clutching the infant protectively to her chest. Shingas spoke again, the same hard tone to his voice.

'Give me the child.' It was not a request.

In desperation Esther turned and looked towards the old squaw seated across from her. Putting down the cradle board, the old squaw met her imploring look and nodded her head reassuringly. Filled with a sense of uncertainty, reluctantly Esther held out the baby, letting Shingas takes the child from her.

With the naked infant held safely in his arms, Shingas walked out from the village and set off through the forest as it climbed away before him. Up and up he went, each slope leading to another even higher one, their craggy sides littered with rocks and the skeletons of fallen trees. Eventually as the forest thinned, shafts of sunlight pierced the canopy like bolts of celestial light through the nave window of a cathedral and with his heart pounding, Shingas reached the final peak, its naked summit crowned with a rocky outcrop of weathered boulders, each one as old as Christendom. Jutting out from amongst them like a cantilevered balcony, was a single giant slab of granite. A promontory so precariously balanced that it seemed it only needed a butterfly to settle on its tip to send it toppling into the void below.

With the wind swirling about him, Shingas stepped out onto the granite slab, its surface as flat and smooth as a table top and standing like a figure cast in bronze, feet firmly planted, his arms outstretched, he held the naked infant aloft. Stretching before and below them as far as the eye could see was an unbroken panorama of forest-covered mountains, an unending wilderness set with great valleys and lakes, the world as God created it, and the home of the Seneca.

With the evening shadows lengthening and the baby none the worst for its lengthy outing, Shingas returned to the long-house. Entering their compartment and finding Esther stretched out on a bed of furs, seemingly asleep Shingas lay down on the cot opposite. With the contented infant cradled gently in the crook of his arm, lost in devotion he gazed down on his son as his tiny hands took an interest in the bear-claw necklace around his neck. Unnoticed, peering through half-open eyes, Esther looked on in disbelief at the tenderness of the scene, hardly daring to believe what she was witnessing. Amazed that this savage whom she feared and hated could be capable of such love was almost beyond her comprehension.

Moments later a warrior appeared in the doorway and the spell was broken. Covering the baby with a fur blanket, Shingas snatched up his musket and quietly slipped away. After waiting a moment to be sure that he had gone, Esther climbed up from her cot and pulling down the top of her dress, she picked up the infant and held him to her breast, watching with satisfaction as the hungry infant clamped his mouth around her swollen nipple and began sucking on it voraciously.

CHAPTER ELEVEN

O N THE 28TH July, after resting for a further day while additional supplies of flour were sent out from Carlisle, fifty miles to the east, Colonel Bouquet's small army of no more than five hundred men were at last ready to depart on their undertaking. With a bright morning sun already warming the air, accompanied by the insistent rattle of a kettledrum the Grenadiers and Highlanders broke camp and began forming up in their ranks.

At the centre of the convoy, flanked on both sides by a company of Light Infantry, the heavy wagons, drawn by teams of oxen were brought into line. Behind them a small herd of cattle were kept in check by half a dozen stick wielding drovers. Finally, strung out in a long line came the pack-horses their dancing hooves throwing up clouds of dust and inciting curses from the rear-guard of Grenadiers as it clogged their nostrils and settled on their blood-red jackets.

At the head of the column, seated astride their well-schooled mounts, Colonel Bouquet and his officers, fortified by a hearty breakfast of cold ham and poached eggs, washed down by cups of steaming coffee, watched proceedings with a critical eye. Also looking on but with less interest, were a group of thirty or so backwoodsmen, who by good fortune Colonel Bouquet had at last managed to engage. Dressed in their usual fringed hunting-frocks and resting lazily on the barrel of their flintlock musket they viewed the scene of orderly chaos with an air of bored indifference. Standing in their midst, as though wishing to be inconspicuous, were Samuel and Adam Endicote.

Advised by the company sergeants that all was ready, Colonel Bouquet threw a farewell salute to Captain Ourry looking down from the forts ramparts like a king in his castle. Then kicking his horse into a walk and surrounded by his covey of officers, he led his army out from the small settlement. Lining the street, if a dusty track could be given such a title, the crowd of displaced settlers, who had gathered to witness their departure, gazed in anxious silence as the column tramped its way towards the surrounding wilderness. Watching until with a last glimpse of scarlet jacket, it disappeared beneath the evergreen arches of the forest and was lost from sight.

After an hour into the march and judging that the wild nature of the country offered an ideal opportunity for an enemy to ambush them. Colonel Bouquet gave the order for a party of the backwoodsmen to be sent ahead of the column to scout the woods for danger. The remainder he posted as a rear-guard behind the company of Grenadiers guarding the train of pack-horses. With these steps taken to secure them from any surprise attack the convoy of troops and wagons, surrounded on all sides by an impervious wall of trees and foliage, trudged along the rugged track that was the Forbes Road.

On the fifth day Colonel Bouquet's little army reached the main ridge of the Alleghany mountains and began the long climb towards its peak. Hour after hour they slogged up its densely wooded heights, zigzagging around rocky outcrops and the decaying trunks of fallen trees. The oxen panting as they drew the heavy wagons over the torturous terrain and every soldier cursing the thickness of his uniforms as they sweated in the July heat. At long last, after two days they reached the summit and to a man they stood gazing in awe at the view before and below them. An unending wilderness of forest covered mountains stretching on forever, their verdant slopes dappled by a passing armada of billowing clouds.

After descending the ridge, thankfully the country became less rugged and the woods less dense and without rocks and half buried stumps to impede the wagons, they made good time. On the sixth day, after stopping to rest and water the stock at a small stream, they at last reached the little outpost of Fort Ligonier. Constructed in 1758 and positioned on a low hill beside the Loyalhanna Creek, some fifty miles from Fort Bedford, the outposts principal purpose was to protect the passage of supplies onwards to Fort Pitt situated at the confluence of the Alleghany and the Monogahela rivers. Although smaller in size than Fort Bedford its high walls set in a square with a roofed bastion at each corner gave it a formidable appearance. Lying outside the fort, and encircled by a deep ditch were a cluster of sturdy outbuildings, comprising of a saw mill, a smoke-house and a forge. Entered by a central gateway defended by a wooden palisade, the fort's spacious interior boasted an officers' mess, a guardhouse, a quartermaster's store and a large barracks. Glad though they were to set eyes on its ramparts, what pleased Bouquet's weary troops more was the sight of the cross of St George fluttering atop its flagpole.

Waiting at the gates, as welcome to see such a large body of troops as they themselves were to have reached the safety of the outpost, was the fort's commander, Lieutenant Archibald Blane a doughy scot and an officer known to Colonel Bouquet. A month previously the former had angered Bouquet by intimating that he should abandon the fort. Since then however, his resolute actions in defending the post against attack by the marauding Indians with only a garrison of seven soldiers, had restored the Colonel's faith in the officer's integrity and so assured a cordial meeting between the two. After exchanging a customary salute, Colonel Bouquet dismounted and the two officers shook hands. Eager for news it was Colonel Bouquet who spoke first.

'Did the reinforcements I dispatched arrive safely?'

'Indeed they did sir and never was I so glad to see a tartan kilt or to welcome such fine soldiers.'

'Then all is well?'

'Aye Colonel all is well. There have been but two attacks, the second on the twenty first being by far the most serious with upwards of one thousand shots being fired by the enemy.'

'Do you have casualties?'

'None sir. It would appear that my good fortune in times of danger still attends me.'

'Excellent! But tell me pray what news of Fort Pitt?'

'On that question sir I have only bad news having heard nothing from them since the thirtieth of May. Though two expresses have gone through from Bedford not one has returned.'

Clearly disturbed by this news, Colonel Bouquet swallowed his disappointment, concerning himself instead with the safety of his men and supplies.

'Have you room inside for my wagons and horses?'

'Indeed Colonel and space in the barracks for some of your men should you need it, for I am certain they would welcome a cot after so many nights spent lying on the hard ground.'

Although touched by the intended kindness of Blane's suggestion, Colonel Bouquet's reply was quite brusque.

'Thank you but no sir. The men are quite used to their tents and weary as they surely are, the hard ground will not cause them to lose sleep.' Then in a lighter tone but spoken more as an intention than a request, he went on, 'But if you've no objection, my officers and I will accommodate ourselves in your officers' quarters.'

With matters settled between them and after receiving reports from his officers that his wishes for the safety and welfare of his force had been carried out, Colonel Bouquet retired to his allotted quarters. Although more weary than he would care to admit, the reason was more to achieve a period of solitude than to seek some rest, for there was much to occupy his mind. Although Fort Pitt was less than three days march away, the perilous route which lay ahead and the very real possibility of an ambush, consumed his thoughts.

An hour or so later, with his mind clear of worries and his plans for the following days in order, Colonel Bouquet left his quarters. Passing by the oxen and horses corralled behind the heavy wagons, some already asleep on their feet, he climbed the ladder up to the walk-way connecting the two bastions which faced towards the creek. With a nod to the sentry on duty, who jumped smartly to attention, he strolled along the narrow platform. The golden disc of the sun was beginning its descent in the western sky and a warm breeze tugged at the flag of St George. Stopping at length he gazed down on the neat rows of tents below, with the soldier's muskets propped like sheaves of corn beside them. Standing alone in the silence, the soft murmur of voices carried up to him, causing a smile of amusement to cross his face. It seemed that no matter how weary they were after a gruelling day's march, there were still some souls who found the energy for conversation. Turning away, his heart filled with admiration for the uncomplaining nature of his men, he prayed that with God's good grace they would all be safely delivered to Fort Pitt.

With the tempting aroma of roasting meat in his nostrils, prompted by hunger, Colonel Bouquet made his way to the mess which adjoined the officers' quarters. Entering the room, the off duty officers seated around the long table quickly jumped to their feet. Acknowledging the officers with a brief nod of the head, Colonel Bouquet took his place at the table. With the Colonel seated, two orderlies entered the room, one carrying a tray laden with a large joint of roast beef, the other an open tureen piled high with steaming potatoes. Setting them down on the table, without a word they turned about and left the room. Climbing to his feet a young Lieutenant of the Seventy Seventh regiment quickly snatched up the meat fork and carving knife strategically placed on either side of the joint and turning to face Colonel Bouquet he asked.

'With your permission sir?'

Smiling at the young officer's undisguised eagerness, Colonel Bouquet gave a permissive wave of his hand, watching in amusement as the young officer attacked the joint more with enthusiasm than skill. Spurring him on, his fellow officers, irrespective of rank and with little regard for propriety, struck the table with their pewter plates, and demanded the first slice.

With the meal concluded and all three bottles of Lieutenant Blane's fine claret empty, Colonel Bouquet, took up his fork and banging the bone handle down hard on the table, he brought the room to order.

'Gentlemen your attention.' Pausing for a moment until all eyes were on him Colonel Bouquet then continued,

'Given that no news has been received from Fort Pitt and with little intelligence concerning the enemy and their whereabouts, I have resolved to press on with all haste. In order to do so it is my intention to leave behind the oxen and wagons and to carry such supplies as we may need and all the flour, on pack-horses.'

As a demonstration of their trust and confidence in their commanding officer, his decision was greeted by a unanimous nodding of heads.

'Furthermore given that our route of march will take us through the treacherous pass at Turtle Creek and aware of the opportunity the spot offers for ambush, I propose that we march as far as Bushy Run. Once there we will rest until nightfall and then under cover of darkness, cross Turtle Creek by a forced march. Are there any questions?'

The first to respond was Lieutenant Blane and getting to his feet he asked.

'What of my reinforcements Colonel, am I to keep them?'

Colonel Bouquet's reply was firm but uncompromising.

'Yes Lieutenant but since I cannot risk reducing my force, from necessity they will be fewer in number and made up of those who are judged too infirm to endure the march ahead.'

Feeling somewhat hard done by, but knowing that there was little point in raising an objection, Lieutenant Blane returned to his chair.

Throwing a look around the table and seeing that there were to be no more questions, Colonel Bouquet pushed back his seat and accompanied by the scraping of chair legs, as the officers around the table quickly clambered to their feet, he got up from the table.

'It has been a tiring day, so if you gentlemen will excuse me I must retire to my bed.' Before turning away, smiling benignly, he added in a parental manner. 'After such a copious meal and with Lieutenant Blane's fine claret drained to the last drop, might I suggest that you may also consider following my example?'

Next morning after allowing a late breakfast for his men and seeing an express-rider sent on his way with a despatch for Sir Jeffrey Amherst, Colonel Bouquet and his little force, together with three hundred and fifty pack-horses and a few cattle, set out on the final leg of their march to Fort Pitt. With Turtle Creek two days march away after covering less than a dozen miles, much to the surprise and delight of the troops who were more used to tramping twice the distance in a day, Colonel Bouquet calling a halt and ordering an early camp to be made. At dawn camp was struck and the march to Bushy Run, some twenty miles ahead, where Bouquet intended to rest until nightfall before pushing on across Turtle Creek under cover of darkness, was resumed. All that day, strung out in a long line and sweltering in the heat, men and horses slogged along the narrow road as it lead them up and down the backs of densely wooded hills. Ahead of the column as always were the advance guard of Backwoodsmen and Highlanders with the remaining Backwoodsmen bringing up the rear. Among these were Samuel Endicote and his son Adam, following his father like a faithful hound. Although outwardly his physical appearance had remained the same, except perhaps for a gauntness to his face that was not evident before, inside Samuel's very being burned with an all-consuming hatred of Indians and a desire for revenge so strong that it possessed his very soul. Powerless to act alone, to dispel the rage of frustration and to give his life a purpose, he had seized on the chance to join Colonel Bouquets army and although unsure how the enterprise would fulfil his thirst for vengeance, given its purpose, he was certain that an opportunity to slake it would arise.

Perhaps if he had been among those scouring the woods up ahead and if he had possessed the eyesight of a hawk, unwittingly he might well have glimpsed the cause of his hatred manifested before him. For watching from a high vantage point, surrounded by dense foliage, Shingas and a small group of warriors, their faces daubed with fresh war-paint, peered down at Colonel Bouquet and his troops as they made their way slowly towards them through the verdant forest like a snake moving through tall grass. Turning away from the scene below him, Shingas gave his instructions, and watched with grim satisfaction as three of the group turned and melted away into the trees, eager to carry his words to the warriors' waiting below.

Riding at the head of the column and flanked by several of his officers, after a tiring day in the saddle, Colonel Bouquet was pleased to receive news from one of the Backwoodsmen who had been sent to scout ahead, that Bushy Run was less than half a mile away. With little time for the pomposity exhibited by many of his English counterparts, Colonel Bouquet turned his horse and riding along the line of weary soldiers, who had foot-slogged for twenty miles without rest, cursing and sweating in the sweltering heat, he called out in a cheery voice.

'A few yards more my lads and you shall have the rest you deserve.'

No sooner had the words escaped his lips when from up ahead came the sharp rattle of gunfire, sending a ripple of excitement along the ranks. Spurring his horse to the head of the line, Colonel Bouquet listened as the firing intensified and mingled in with it, the unmistakable sound of Indian war-cries.

With the column halted on the crest of a low hill, Colonel Bouquet ordered Lieutenant McIntosh forward with two companies of Light Infantry from the 42nd regiment to support the advance guard, watching with some anxiety as they disappeared into the woods. Within a few minutes, his fears were realised as rather than dropping away, the sound of musket fire increased. Grim faced, soldiers and drivers listened with growing concern to the sounds of battle. Calmly, Colonel Bouquet gathered his mounted officers around him and issued his orders.

Immediately, Captain Lieutenant Graham wheeled his horse around and calling out, he ordered two companies of Grenadiers to fall in as flankers alongside the supply-convoy. As the Grenadiers broke ranks, the imposing figure of Major Campbell, mounted on his grey horse formed the remaining troops into an extended line and the order was given to fix bayonets.

Up ahead, unable to advance or retreat, with the dead and wounded laying where they had fallen, the advance guard of Backwoodsmen and Highlanders, supported by the two companies of Light Infantry were pinned down by heavy gunfire. Seeking what cover they could find amongst the scattered trees they returned fire. The Backwoodsmen firing only when a target presented itself, while Lieutenant McIntosh's Light Infantry responded with co-ordinated but ineffective volleys which spattered harmlessly among the trees. Fearing for their lives as the firing from the enemy increased, the advanced guard were greatly relieved when suddenly from behind them a solid line of Highlanders and Grenadiers charged forward through the trees with their mounted officers in the rear, swords in hand, urging them on.

Concealed behind trees and bushes Shingas and a hundred warriors watched as the line of soldiers clambered up the sloping ground towards them their uniforms conspicuous among the green foliage, their bayonets glinting in the occasional shafts of sunlight. Choosing their moment, the Indians leapt from cover and poured a heavy fire into the advancing soldiers, immediately falling back into cover among the crowded trees. Below them the line staggered under the wasting volley and scores of soldiers were hit and fell to the ground. Quickly the gaps were filled and without wavering the soldiers continued their advance up the wooded hillside, the Highlanders among them screaming like banshees. Ahead of them, with no time to reload their muskets, the Indians abandoned their positions and like spectres they melted away into the woods. With the ridge cleared of the enemy, a great cheer went up from Highlanders and Grenadiers alike and the charge was halted. But even as they celebrated their success, from the rear came the crash of musket fire and the shriek of war-cries and fearing that the convoy would be lost the order was given to fall back.

With his warriors crowded around him, their muskets reloaded and impatient to renew the fight, Shingas watched with satisfaction as the soldiers began to withdraw. Leaping to his feet with a guttural cry he urged his warriors to attack and like hounds freed from the leash, the Indians bounded forward down the slope and emptied their muskets into the ranks of the retreating soldiers.

With the supply-convoy now under his command, Captain Lieutenant Graham rode his horse along the line, urging the drivers to bring their strings of pack-horses alongside each other in order to shorten the line and make it easier for his two companies of Grenadiers to defend. No sooner had the drivers begun the manoeuvre when the rattle of gunfire erupted on both sides and a storm of bullets flew among them, striking men and horses alike. Unperturbed by the ensuing panic among the drivers, Lieutenant Graham ordered his Grenadiers to form into ranks along both flanks of the convoy. With practised ease the soldiers took up position, their muskets at the ready. Pistol in hand, the young officer shouted out above the din.

'Fire!'

Immediately the muskets of the Grenadiers exploded in a deafening volley.

Meanwhile, following their Colonels orders, grudgingly the Grenadiers and Highlanders, some of them supporting a wounded comrade, fell back towards the beleaguered supply-convoy. Snapping at their heels like a pack of hungry wolves

Shingas and his warriors followed stopping only to scalp the dead and dying soldiers who lay where they had fallen and stripping them of their weapons.

Major Campbell, with a hole in the sleeve of his scarlet uniform where a musket ball had passed through, was the first officer to reach the supply-convoy. Seeing Pahotan and a pack of Seneca warriors closing on the hard pressed Grenadiers, he spurred his horse forward. Spotting a body of Highlanders emerging from the forest, he turned in the saddle and ordered them forward. Needing no encouragement and yelling at the tops of their voices, the Highlanders charged forward, their bayonets thirsty for blood. Seeing that he was out-numbered, Pahotan shouted out to his warriors and once aware of the danger, they turned and fled into the surrounding woods.

With the supply-convoy secure from immediate danger and thankful for the lack of a sustained attack by his savage enemies, Colonel Bouquet gave the order for his troops to form a defensive ring around the convoy of terrified pack-horses. Immediately, directed by their mounted officers, the Highlanders, Grenadiers and Light Infantry quickly encircled an area of ground large enough to accommodate the beleaguered convoy. At its centre, seemingly oblivious to the bullets flying in from all directions, a party of Backwoodsmen began preparing a defensive position as a sanctuary for the wounded by stripping flour-bags from the pack-horses and piling them one on top of the other, into a barricade of sorts.

Galled, Shingas watched as the redcoats began organising their defensive ring, angry that the combined force of Seneca, Delaware and Shawnee had not continued with the attack while the enemy were unprepared. But without an overall commander, each tribe being led by their own war-chief, and without a coherent strategy, the opportunity had been missed. In his heart though he knew that all was not lost, for although the Yenge army was their equal in numbers, this method of warfare, of surprise attacks, striking swiftly at the enemy and then melting away, was well suited to this wilderness of forest and hills and totally alien to their encircled enemy. Their forte was the European ideal of open fields of battle, where opposing armies, resplendent in their colourful uniforms, with standards unfurled and the boom of cannon in their ears, faced each other, drawn up in extended ranks. And this he knew would be their downfall. Even as the party of Backwoodsmen laboured over their walls of flour-bags, Pahotan and a combined force of Seneca and Delaware warriors moved cautiously forward through the crowded trees. At Pahotan's side was Custaloga, a Delaware war-chief, his long, black flowing hair crested with ravens feathers, his cheeks daubed with vermilion and ochre. Resting lightly in the hollow of his arm was a fearsome looking war-club.

As an uneasy calm descended, seizing on the lull in the battle, the wounded were carried from the line and placed behind the protective wall of flour-bags. Those who remained at their station waited grim-faced for the expected attack. Behind them, the herd of restless horses, their ears pricked, nostrils flared, stood crowded together, held in check by their nervous drivers.

Samuel and half a dozen Backwoodsmen settled themselves in behind a fallen tree close to the crest of the hill and with a good view to their front they waited, eager for the chance to send a musket ball into any savage who showed himself. Obedient to his father's wishes, Adam remained inside the protective square of flour-bags, the wounded stretched out on the ground around him, passive and helpless. Samuel had already lost three of his four sons to these heathen devils, he would not let them take the last of them.

Suddenly the silence was shattered by a war-cry and Custaloga and his Delaware warriors burst out from the surrounding forest, and charging forward whooping and yelling towards the line of soldiers, they poured a murderous fire into their ranks and then with great agility, took cover among the crowded trees. A number of soldiers were hit and went down, while the remainder, without need of an order, fired a volley into the trees. Led by Captain Bassett they then closed ranks and charged forward with fixed bayonets, screaming their defiance. Without waiting to receive the attack, Custaloga and his warriors, their copper-skinned bodies acting as a natural camouflage, melted away into the trees and vanished from sight.

Returning to their position, having been frustrated again by the enemy's tactics, suddenly without warning, Pahotan and his Seneca warriors rushed out from among the trees on their flank and sent a wasting volley of musket balls and arrows into their ranks. Caught in the hail of missiles, Captain Lieutenant Graham's horse was shot from under him. Beside him, a Grenadier silently slumped to the ground, a feathered shaft protruding from his left eye. Immediately another soldier stepped up and took his place and the gap in the ranks was filled. His face contorted with rage, his scream as wild as any Highlander, sword in hand, Captain Bassett, lead the remaining soldiers in a bayonet charge. Behind him, the dead and wounded soldiers were removed from the line.

At the crest of the low hill crouching behind their barricade, grim faced, Samuel and the Backwoodsmen fired at will, each taking silent pleasure when they saw their shot strike home. Numb with terror and with the bodies of the wounded crowded around him bandaged and bleeding, Adam pressed himself into a corner of the makeshift wall, his hands clamped over his ears to shut out their plaintive cries for water.

After fighting without respite for over seven hours, with night's inky darkness as arbiter the firing from both sides subsided and eventually dropped away. Seizing the opportunity, the exhausted soldiers, desperate for rest, slumped to the ground where they stood. Conscious of the importance of morale, their officers moved amongst them, offering words of praise for their discipline and steadfastness. With sentries posted against a surprise night attack and fearful of lighting fires the camp settled into an uneasy night. Occasionally the men's fitful sleep was broken by a wild yell from the forest, a reminder of what awaited them when the cloak of darkness was lifted.

With the camp settled and secure, Colonel Bouquet retired to the small tent which had been erected for him alongside the barricade of flour-bags. Pen in hand, by the light of a guttering candle he began writing of the day's events and of his fears for tomorrow in a despatch to Sir Jeffrey Amhurst, concluding with;

> *We also suffered considerably: Capt. Liet.*
> *Graham and Liet. James McIntosh of the 42nd are*
> *killed and Capt. Graham wounded. Of the Royal*
> *American Regt. Lieut. Dow is shot through the*
> *body. Of the 77th Lieut. Donald Campbell and*
> *Mr Peebles, a volunteer, are wounded. Our loss*
> *in men, including Backwoodsmen and drivers,*
> *exceeds sixty killed or wounded. The action has*
> *lasted from one O'clock 'till night and we expect*
> *to begin again at day break. Whatever our*
> *fate may be, I thought it necessary to give your*
> *Excellency this early information, that you may*
> *at all events, take such measures as you will think*
> *proper with the Provinces, for their own safety*
> *and the effectual relief of Fort Pitt, as in case*

of another engagement I fear insurmountable difficulties in protecting and transporting our provisions, being already so much weakened by the losses of the day, in men and horses: besides the additional necessity of carrying the wounded, whose situation is truly deplorable.

I cannot sufficiently acknowledge the constant assistance I have received from Major Campbell during the long action; nor express my admiration for the cool and steady behaviour of the troops, who did not fire a shot without orders and drove the enemy from their posts with fixed bayonets. The conduct of the Officers is much above my praises.

I have the Honour to be, with great respect, Sir & ca.
Henry Bouquet.

Woken by the sound of a dawn chorus such as they had never heard before, the soldiers climbed wearily to their feet, the deafening crash of muskets and the war-cries of their savage enemy ringing in their ears. Seeking what cover they could find against the hail of deadly missiles they calmly took post, expecting an assault at any moment but at a loss to know which direction it might come from.

Their expectations were quickly realised when at the foot of the low hill, silent and unseen among the surrounding trees, Shingas and a large body of Seneca warriors approached to within a hundred feet of the thin line of troops. Levelling their muskets, with a shout from Shingas they poured a heavy fire into the defenders. Then with the flash and smoke of exploding muskets and the stench of gunpowder filling the air, brandishing their tomahawks they raced out from the cover of the encircling woods. Screaming their war-whoops they fell on their hated enemy, hacking at the wounded laying helpless on the ground and forcing back the hard pressed survivors.

Spotting the danger, Captain Bassett rallied a company of Highlanders to him and with his trusty sword gripped in his hand, he led them in a charge down the slope. Seeing the reinforcements bearing down on them, Shingas called off the attack and with his warriors, many of them carrying a bloody trophy, he retreated back into the safety of the trees, those with a loaded musket firing a parting shot at the advancing Highlanders.

No sooner was the breach in the defensive circle filled when from every side, parties of Shawnee and Delaware rushed up and screaming their war-cries they fell with increased ferocity on the defenders, desperate to break into the circle. Inside the camp itself, crowded together against the wall of flour-bags, scores of horses, terrified by the shrieks and yells of the Indians and the crash of muskets, suddenly broke free and with thundering hooves they burst through the ring of troops and raced away into the encircling forest.

Conscious of the importance of securing the pack-horses and oblivious to the bullets flying around him, Major Campbell rode across to the group of drivers cowering against the wall of sacks and bellowed at them to control their animals. But his order fell on deaf ears as overcome by fear, many of them simply ignored him while others, filled with terror ran off seeking what cover they could among the trees and bushes. Pulling on his reigns, Major Campbell turned away in disgust and as he did so, his mount suddenly let out a whinnying scream and dropped onto its knees its huge liquid eyes wide with fear. Sliding free from the saddle the major watched in horror as with every heartbeat the horse's life-blood began pumping from the bullet wounds in its neck and forming a puddle on the dry ground. A ribbon of blood which slowly flowed outwards creating a crimson halo around its noble head.

All morning the fight raged and despite being wearied by fatigue and thirst, having been without water since the previous morning, the battle-weary troops still held their defensive circle around the convoy. Looking on from his position at the heart of the camp and seeing a growing number of his gallant soldiers falling in their ranks, Colonel Bouquet sensed the tide of battle was turning against them. Determined to reverse their fortunes, he quickly gathered his officers around him and with bullets droning past like angry bees, in a rising voice, he informed them of his plan.

'Gentlemen, I fear gallantry alone will not win us this fight. Indeed if all is not to be lost the savages must be made to stand their ground and fight.'

The ring of officers listened, grim-faced.

'And since from want of numbers we cannot attack them, lest we place our wounded in great danger. I intend a strategy to bring the enemy to us.'

Turning to face Major Campbell; an officer in his thirties with an aquiline nose and dark hooded eyes, he went on. 'Major Campbell, on my word you are to withdraw a company of Light Infantry from the line and a company of Highlanders from the 42nd. The troops on each flank will then be required to pull back and close ranks to fill the gap. It is my hope that the savages will mistake this as a sign that we intend to retreat and become so filled with confidence that they will attack us in force.'

Pausing while a sergeant with a blood stained bandage around his head and a dozen soldiers ran past them, he continued, a growing urgency in his voice.

'You and your men are then to take a position to the left of the line where the enemy cannot observe you and if the strategy works, you are to choose the most auspicious moment and fall upon their right flank.'

Major Campbell nodded his head in affirmation. Turning to Captain Bassett, Colonel Bouquet fixed him with a steady stare.

'You sir with the Third Light Infantry Company and the Grenadiers of the 42nd will take up such a position that at the first favourable moment you can add your support to the attack.'

With a last look at the circle of faces surrounding him, Colonel Bouquet concluded.

'I fear that we shall only have one chance at it gentlemen, so strike them hard and show no mercy.'

With the order given, Major Campbell began withdrawing the two companies from the line, while one either side, his two Lieutenants pulled back the troops on both flanks until the breach was filled. Meanwhile, in the rear, Captain Bassett moved away with his companies of Light Infantry and Grenadiers, the naked steel of their bayonets glinting in the shafts of morning sunlight. With hopes of being unobserved, he lead them into a shallow depression between two low hills, one of which overlooked the right flank of Major Campbell's force. Once in position, he settled down to wait the outcome of Colonels Bouquet's audacious plan.

From the encircling forest Pahotan and Custaloga watched with mounting interest as the soldiers withdrew from their position and retreated towards the centre of the camp. With so few soldiers left to oppose them, filled with confidence the two war-chiefs signalled to their waiting warriors, drawing them closer. Moments later a hundred Seneca and Delaware warriors poured a volley of musket fire and arrows into the thin line of troops. Then armed with tomahawks and war-clubs they charged out from the trees and with their chilling war-cries resounding through the forest they fell upon the desperately outnumbered soldiers.

Overwhelmed, their meagre wall of bayonets of little protection against the Indians' savage onslaught, the thin line of soldiers was slowly forced back, their dead and wounded left to the mercy of the scalping knife. With the line breached the Indians pressed forward, eager to put their hated enemy under the knife until not a single soldier was left alive.

Watching with satisfaction as the enemy swallowed the bait, Major Campbell advanced his two companies to the crest of the low ridge which had concealed them. Allowing a moment for his men to level their muskets and take aim, he raised his sword and roared out.

'Fire!'

Instantly a crashing volley echoed through the trees and a hail of musket balls scythed into the attacking Indians, killing many of them and wounding many more. Stunned by the attack, the surviving Seneca and Delaware warriors turned to face this new danger, watching in horror as Major Campbell clamboured to his feet and pointing the blade of his sword towards them yelled out at the top of his voice.

'Charge!'

Consumed with frustration at having to endure a battle fought entirely under conditions imposed on them by their elusive enemy. Given a chance to fight on their own terms, screaming their blood curdling battle cries, the wild Highlanders and the company of Light Infantry charged down the slope and fell on the Indians with their bayonets.

Screaming his war-cry Pahotan turned to face the charging soldiers. Others around him, recovering from the surprise of the attack, followed his example and clutching their tomahawks and war-clubs they readied themselves for the soldiers' onslaught. But the shock was too much, the bayonets too irresistible and after a brief resistance, panic spread through the surviving warriors like flames through dry grass and as one they turned and fled. Caught in the melee, Pahotan lashed out at the soldier in front of him, the wicked curve of his tomahawk's steel head sinking into the man's face, slicing through cartilage and bone destroying his face and dropping him dying onto his knees. Freeing his axe, Pahotan turned to face his next assailant. But even as he caught sight of him it was too late and with a primeval yell the Highlander plunged his bayonet deep into Pahotan's chest, the force of the thrust driving the war-chief backwards onto the ground. Wrenching the twelve inches of steel free, his face contorted with hatred, the soldier lunged forward again and with Pahotan lying helpless on his back, he drove the bloodied blade into the dying warrior's exposed throat.

With the din of the fight loud in his ears Captain Bassett led his men to the crest of the low hill overlooking Major Campbell's flank and formed them into two ranks. No sooner had the soldiers taken station when the routed Indians raced past directly in front of them. Although eager to discharge their muskets, the soldiers waited for their officer's command. Admiring his men's steadfast behaviour, judging the moment, Captain Bassett gave the command to fire. Instantly, the soldiers poured a heavy volley into the fleeing Indians, watching with grim satisfaction as many of them flung up their arms and tumbled to the ground, either dead or wounded.

From his vantage point, confronted by the unbroken defensive ring of soldiers and powerless to go to their aid, Shingas watched

186

as the surviving Seneca and Delaware warriors, hard pressed by the pursuing Highlanders, fled into the safety of the woods. Knowing all was lost but without allowing the bitterness of defeat to manifest itself upon his face, Shingas gathered his remaining warriors about him and led them away into the safety of the forest.

With the camp secure and their enemy defeated, the exhausted soldiers sent up a great cheer when their victorious comrades returned from pursuing the Indians and driving them from the surrounding woods. Two of the Highlanders had caught one of the fleeing savages and dragging him forward they threw him onto the ground in front of the assembled defenders. Immediately, pistol in hand, Major Campbell strode forward and calmly raising his weapon he despatched the hapless prisoner with a shot through the head as though he were a rabid dog.

With the woods cleared of the enemy Colonel Bouquet gave instruction for litters to be prepared for the wounded and such stores and flour as could not be carried on the few horses left to them, to be burned. With these matters attended to and in the relative calm following the aftermath of the battle he once more put pen to paper in a despatch to his commanding officer. Writing of the day's events in concise terms and speaking modestly of his own part in the victory, he sighted the losses among his force during the two days of battle as eight officers and one hundred and fifteen men killed. From necessity the unenviable task of listing their names must wait for a more opportune time. He concluded as always with praise for his troops by saying, 'That on this occasion, their behaviour speaks for itself so strongly that for me to attempt to eulogise further, would but detract from their merit.'

CHAPTER TWELVE

D ETERMINED TO PUNISH those tribes responsible for the attacks on His Majesty's forts and settlements and to subjugate them utterly and completely. With Fort Pitt now secure and reinforced by a force of a thousand provincial troops, raised and authorised by the Pennsylvania Assembly and with the remnants of his own regulars and those Backwoodsmen who had chosen to remain now suitably rested, Colonel Bouquet was ready to march westwards into a wilderness where no army had ventured before.

With his troops lined up in their ranks and his convoy of pack-horse laden with supplies and a herd of cattle and flock of sheep, brought along to provide meat, assembled, Colonel Bouquet began his march. Crossing over the Allegheny river and without a road of any sort to follow, where the terrain dictated it, scores of engineers and axemen were employed to hack a path through the wall of trees, while ahead of them the Backwoodsmen, who Colonel Bouquet held in high regard, scouted the forest for signs of ambush. Toiling through the seemingly unending wilderness of dark woods and tangled thickets, making at best little more than eight miles a day, slowly but inexorably the army of retribution made its way down the Ohio valley with its vistas of unspeakable majesty and deeper into the enemies' heartland.

Occasionally they would encounter the broad expanse of the Ohio river and for as long as was possible they would march along beside its slowly eddying current enjoying the brightness of the grassy margins along its wide shore and the welcome shade offered by the groves of maple and basswood. On the tenth day of their march they reached the banks of the Muskingum River, deep inside their enemys' homeland and after following its serpentine course for several miles, finding a suitable fording-place, they crossed to the western bank and made camp.

Next morning a few Indians were seen skulking around the edges of the surrounding woods but seeing the vast number of troops before them, they quickly disappeared. Continuing down the wooded valley of the Muskingum, after marching a few miles the army came across an abandoned Tuscarora village. Although there was little need to announce the arrival of his troops, seizing on the opportunity to increase the Indians fears and much to the delight of his men, Colonel Bouquet ordered that it should be burned to the ground. Well into the afternoon Bouquet's army of retribution reached a wide meadow bordered by broken woodland. Judging it a suitable spot for an encampment, with grazing for his animals and a ready source of firewood Colonel Bouquet ordered a halt. Later, after setting his engineers and axemen to work constructing a palisade in which the stores could be kept secure and with fire-pits dug and cooks and butchers already preparing for the evening meal, Colonel Bouquet convened a meeting with his officers, and speaking without pomp or ceremony he ensured that all present were left in no doubt as to his intentions in dealing with their savage opponents. He then ordered that the twenty of so Mohawk Indians, sent to him as guides and interpreters by Sir William Johnson, should be despatched to the surrounding villages of the Shawnee and Delaware. Their mission being to deliver his demand that their chiefs should meet him next day on the meadow bordering the river below the camp.

The following morning, with a watery sun blessing the occasion with its presence, Colonel Bouquet's troops, accompanied by the rattle of drums, moved in battle order onto the meadow. In perfect formation they tramped through the dew laden grass their bayonets gleaming in the brightening light, and formed up in two extended lines. The Highlanders in their tartan kilts, the Royal Americans in their scarlet coats and the Provincial Levies in their dull blue jackets and red waistcoats, setting a scene of military might clearly intended to both impress and strike fear into the hearts of their enemy.

At the centre of the meadow beneath a rustic arbour constructed the previous day from saplings and wooden boughs, Colonel Bouquet and the most senior amongst his officers seated on chairs carried by wagon from Fort Pitt for this occasion, watching with pride as the soldiers paraded before them. The former noting with pleasure that, grouped at the end of the line, the party of Backwoodsmen, dressed in their familiar fringed hunting-shirts with their muskets carried in the crook of their arms, had chosen to attend.

At the appointed hour, a delegation of tribal chiefs arrived by canoe from the far bank of the Muskingum and proceeded in imperious fashion between the rows of soldiers towards the arbour. Foremost among them were Custaloga and Kiashuta, dressed in all their finery, each of them wrapped to the throat in a coloured blanket, their bold features painted with ochre and vermilion, white lead and soot. If they were impressed by this show of arms their impervious expressions refused to reveal it.

Seating themselves before the hated English officers, one of the chiefs removed a pipe from beneath his blanket and lit it. With great dignity the pipe was then passed around the circle of delegates, each person, Indian and officer alike, drawing a mouthful of smoke before passing it to the person seated beside him. With the ceremony completed and the pipe placed on the ground between them, Turtle Heart, a Delaware chief climbed to his feet. Clutching a beaded bag containing belts of wampum, he addressed Colonel Bouquet, removing a belt from the bag and placing it before the officer at the conclusion of each sentence.

'Brothers, I speak on behalf of the nations present before you and with this belt I open your ears and your hearts, that you may listen to my words. Brothers, this war was neither our fault nor yours but the work of those nations who live to the westward and their wild young men who would have killed us had we not done their bidding. Brothers, you come amongst us with the hatchet raised to strike us. We now take it from your hand and throw it away. Brothers, it is the will of the Great Spirit that there should be peace between us. We on our side now take hold of the chain of friendship; but as we cannot hold it alone, we desire that you will take hold also and that the Great Spirit will not let it fall from our hands again. Brothers, these words come from our hearts and not our lips. You ask us to return to you all the prisoners amongst us and this we will do, all we ask is that we are given time to do this thing.'

With his lengthy speech concluded, pulling his blanket about him, Turtle Heart seated himself cross-legged onto the ground. No sooner was he seated when one after the other, every chief rose to his feet and voiced his agreement to Turtle Heart's words. Each delivering as he spoke a customary belt of wampum together with a small bundle of sticks indicating the number of prisoners held by each tribe and which they promised to surrender.

With the last tokens placed before him, Colonel Bouquet climbed to his feet. Dispensing with the usual manner of address at such meetings, rather than calling them brothers with its implied overtones of friendship, instead he chose a more formal approach, his strong voice carrying to the ranks of the assembled soldiers.

'Sachems, War-Chiefs the excuses you have offered us are frivolous and unavailing and your conduct is without defence or apology. Your warriors attacked our forts, which were built with your consent and you treacherously destroyed our outposts at Venango and Le Boeuf. Your warriors also assailed our troops, the same troops who now stand before you, in the woods at Bushy Run.'

He paused for a moment, his gaze resting on a young squaw seated at Custaloga's side as delicate as a young fawn, translating his words. When she fell silent, he continued, his tone grave, his words uncompromising.

'We shall endure this no longer and I am now come amongst you to force you to make atonement for the injuries you have done to us.'

The young squaw spoke softly into Custaloga's ear and his eyes flashed with anger.

'Your allies the Ottawa, Ojibwas and Wyandots have begged for peace; the Six Nations have leagued themselves with us; the great lakes and rivers around you are all in our possession and your friends the French are in subjection to us and can do no more to aid you. You are all in our power and if we choose we can exterminate you from the earth.'

The gathered chiefs listened with growing alarm, their faces as imperturbable as always but each of them filled with terror at the sternness of his words.

Waiting a moment for the gravity of his words to sink in, Colonel Bouquet continued, his tone a little softer.

'But the English are a merciful and generous people and if it were possible for you to convince us that you sincerely repent of your past acts and that we could depend on your good behaviour for the future you might yet hope for mercy and peace. If I find that you faithfully execute the conditions, which I shall prescribe I will not treat you with the severity you deserve.'

Pausing briefly to run his eyes over the faces before him Colonel Bouquet went on.

'I give you twelve days from this date, to deliver into my hands all the prisoners in your possession, without exception. Men, women and children whether adopted into your tribes, married or living among you under any denomination or pretence whatsoever. Furthermore you are to furnish them with clothing and provisions sufficient to carry them back to their settlements. When you have complied with these conditions, you shall then learn on what terms you may obtain the peace you desire so much. Furthermore as proof of your intentions I shall require three of your principal chiefs to be given as hostages as security that you will preserve good faith.'

When Colonel Bouquet's words were translated, Custaloga leapt to his feet, his anger and frustration barely concealed. Immediately a file of soldiers, their muskets at the ready, stepped forward and formed a half-circle about the assembled chiefs. With a nod from Colonel Bouquet, Custaloga, Kiashuta and a Shawnee chief were led away by the soldiers.

Watching as the remaining chiefs filed out from beneath the arbour, Colonel Bouquet, a frown forming between his eyes, turned to Captain Bassett seated next to him and said in a voice laced with a modicum of disappointment.

'Alas, for all their fine words I fear that they may yet need some persuasion before my conditions are met.'

Eager as always for action, Captain Bassett seized on his commander's pessimistic comment.

'Perhaps sir, given your misgivings, might not a search of some of their villages provide the encouragement necessary for those who are reluctant to carry out your wishes?'

Inclining his head to conceal the amused expression which had transformed his face, Colonel Bouquet replied in a level tone.

'Very well captain, as you say perhaps a show of arms may well displace any thoughts of leniency they may harbour.'

Smiling broadly, Captain Bassett climbed to his feet and after saluting his colonel he turned and eager to seize the opportunity afforded to him, he strode away, his stride lengthening with every step.

CHAPTER THIRTEEN

A T THE VERY moment that Captain Bassett rode into the village at the head of two companies of red-coated Light Infantry, the old squaw quickly took hold of Esther's hand and hurried away with her to their long-house. Once inside, with a finger to her lips, she pointed to one of the cots. Understanding and hugging the sleeping infant close to her chest Esther lay down on the cot and immediately the old squaw began piling a blanket of furs on top of them, covering them completely. Satisfied that both were hidden, without a word, the old squaw turned and walked away, slipping out of the long-house unnoticed.

Reaching the quadrangle, his excited horse dancing under him, Captain Bassett, every inch the conqueror, swept his impervious gaze over the gathering crowd of Indians and in a loud voice, shouted out his orders to the two company sergeants. Instantly, both NCO's despatched their troops in pairs to begin a search of the village.

Concealed under the blanket of furs, her baby son clutched in her arms Esther heard someone entering the long-house and then the sound of voices, at least two people speaking, their voices although indistinct, clearly not Seneca. Fearful that the frantic beating of her heart would betray them, Esther listened as they drew nearer.

Muskets in hand, the two soldiers moved down the middle of the long-house searching each compartment in turn but without any great conviction, each grumbling in turn at the menial task they had been asigned to. Now and again, to relieve the boredom, they would prod at things with their bayonets, or smash a few earthen ware pots with their heavy boots. Finally, satisfied that they had done enough, they turned about and striding quickly down the wide aisle, thankful to be leaving its gloomy interior, they left the building.

Sitting astride his horse Captain Bassett watched as his troops moved from long-house to long-house searching for prisoners. All around him the large crowd of Seneca, old and young, looked on in anxious silence. Only a few warriors were in evidence and those stood grouped around Wapontak and the elders, their sullen expressions betraying their hatred of the Yenge soldiers. In the forefront of the encircling crowd, Meeataho watched in disbelief as the two soldiers emerged empty-handed from Esther's long-house. Distraught, she pushed free of the throng and rushed across the quadrangle to Captain Bassett and shouting up at him she gestured frantically towards the long-house with her arm. Captain Bassett calmly looked down at her and not understanding a word of what she was saying, he called out to the young Mohawk warrior standing a few feet away.

'You there what is she saying?'

Without waiting for the young Mohawk to reply, Meeataho ran over to the young warrior and pointing towards the long-house from which the two soldiers had emerged, she repeated herself. The young Mohawk listened for a moment then turning towards Captain Bassett and pointing towards the long-house, he translated her words.

'She say white woman in cabin.'

Captain Bassett looked across towards the long-house then asked questioningly.

'Can she be sure?'

The young Mohawk nodded.

'She sure.'

Deliberating for a moment, Captain Bassett turned in his saddle and called out to one of the sergeants.

'Sergeant! Go and search that building again. Thoroughly now do you hear?'

The Sergeant, a man with little time for officers, turned on his heels and without a word, made his way to the long-house and pulling aside the curtain he ducked inside. With a hundred eyes fixed on the doorway, after what seemed an inordinately long time, the sergeant eventually reappeared and holding back the curtain he said something inaudible and blinking in the bright sunlight, Esther emerged from the building, her infant son held in her arms. Looking on, a euphoric Meeataho, her face radiant with triumph, watched as the sergeant took Esther gently by the arm and led her across to Captain Bassett.

Looking down at the woman from his horse and pleased that his suggestion to Colonel Bouquet that such searches should be undertaken, had borne fruit, with a benevolent smile Captain Bassett, said reassuringly.

'Don't be afraid, you're safe now. Your ordeal is over.'

Overwhelmed with emotion, unable to speak, Esther gazed up at the British officer, resplendent in his scarlet jacket with its rows of gleaming gold buttons. Growing impatient at her silence, Captain Bassett leaned forward in the saddle and spoke again, a hint of annoyance in his voice.

'What is your name?" And when she didn't respond, 'can you remember what you are called?'

Struggling for words, Esther finally found her voice.

'Esther Colwill. I am called Esther Colwill.'

Smiling ingeniously Captain Bassett's eyes took in the hybrid infant cradled in her arms.

'And the child, is it yours?'

'Yes the child is mine.'

'And its father, is he here?' Then waving an arm over the surrounding crowd. 'Can you point him out?'

Stung by his words, Esther clutched the infant tightly to her.

'Well,' roared Captain Bassett, 'have you no answer for me?'

'He is not here,' Esther replied, growing a little afraid.

'Is he dead?'

'I don't know sir.'

Rising in the saddle Captain Bassett shouted back at her angrily.

'Killed while attacking His Majesty's soldiers perhaps!'

Shocked, Esther took a step back, the colour draining from her face. Standing close by, the sergeant stared up at the officer with undisguised loathing. Catching the look, embarrassed by his show of temper, Captain Bassett lowered himself into his saddle.

'No matter.'

No sooner had he spoken when a small disturbance in the crowd distracted him and lifting his head he saw a young girl pushing her way through the crowd. Free from the circle of onlookers, she rushed up to Esther and clutched hold of her dress. Smiling, Esther dropped a hand onto Chantal's shoulder and squeezed it gently. Running a gentling hand down his horse's neck, Captain Bassett looked down at the girl, his expression softening a little.

'Well who have we here then? Do you have a name child?'

Chantal gazed up at him with an open face and shrugged her shoulders lightly.

Becoming a little impatient, Captain Bassett asked again.

'Come now child, surely you can tell me your name.'

'She doesn't understand what you are saying.'

Taken unaware by Esther's comment, Captain Bassett looked at her quizzically, puzzled by her remark.

'She is French.'

Stung by Esther's words, Captain Bassett spurred his horse forward and angry at being made to look the fool, he called out.

'Form ranks.' Then jerking on the reins, he swung his mount around and addressed the sergeant. 'Set Mistress Colwill and her infant up on one of the pack-horses.'

With a look towards the girl still clutching tightly onto Esther's dress the sergeant asked.

'And what of the girl sir, are we not to take her too?'

With a face as black as thunder Captain Bassett spat back at him.

'The girl is French sergeant she is no concern of ours.'

Listening to his words in disbelief, Esther cried out.

'No please sir I beg you don't abandon her. I will take care of her, I promise she will be no trouble.'

Rounding on her, Captain Bassett stared down at Esther's anxious face, his eyes deadly, his words laced with bitterness.

'You have your orders sergeant.'

Sensing how useless it would be to protest further, helpless, Esther allowed herself to be led away.

CHAPTER FOURTEEN

F OR TWO DAYS the broad meadow and surrounding woods resounded to the noise of axe and saw. Where once there had been acres of grass, now a good part was occupied by a small town, fortified by a palisade of sharpened stakes and wide ditches banked with earth. Behind these defences, crude cabins had been constructed together with storehouses and a larger cabin to be used as a hospital where any prisoners requiring the attention of a doctor could be administered to. Set about them in orderly rows, were dozens of white military tents. Off to one side a range of low open buildings had also been erected, to serve as temporary housing for those prisoners without family or relatives, until they could be transported back to the settlements in the east.

Facing them a large, open-sided building, thirty feet long and almost as wide, had been constructed, its roof crudely thatched with branches and supported by the upright trunks of young trees set into the ground at regular intervals around its perimeter. Its purpose was to serve as a meeting-house where the prisoners brought in by their Indian captors might be received by those hopeful of catching a glimpse of a loved one who had been snatched from their bosom and thought to be lost to them forever.

On the twelfth day as demanded, they came, crossing the Muskingum in a seemingly endless flotilla of birch-bark canoes crowded with their prisoners. Once across, warriors, some of them carrying a young infant in their strong arms, led their bands of captives up the grassy slope of the meadow towards the meeting-house. Amongst them were troops of wild young children, some of whom had been taken from their natural mothers when they were only babies. Raised as their own by their adoptive parents, they knew nothing other than the Indian way of life. Making up the remainder and outnumbering even the children, were young women, many of whom had become the partners of Indian husbands and carried their hybrid offspring, born to them in captivity.

Awaiting them, crowded together inside the meeting-house, dozens of settlers', mothers and fathers, husbands and brothers strained their eyes, desperately scanning the faces of the approaching captives for a moment of recognition, their hopes and fears resting on a glimpse of a loved one's face.

As they drew closer, a young woman suddenly let out a desperate scream and rushing forward, she snatched a baby from a warrior's arms and clutched it sobbing to her chest. With that the other settlers surged forward and engulfing the prisoners they eagerly searched the faces of those being given up. Bewildered and terrified by the sights and sounds around them and confronted by a sea of strange pale-skinned people, many of the youngsters when they were reunited with their natural mother's, who they had lost all recollection of, simply screamed and struggled to be let free. Equally moving was the sight of those young women, who taken as Indian brides, now stood confronted by fathers and brothers whom they hardly recognised, their emotions a mix of revived memories and feelings of shame for what they had become. Others, having searched desperately among the captives and found no trace of their loved ones, wailed aloud in despair. Several mothers who had lost their offspring as babies years before, knelt in front of a young child frantically scanning its sunburnt face in an agony of hope and doubt.

Spectators to the tragic drama unfolding before them, the battle hardened soldiers deployed about the building, looked on, their emotions concealed behind stoic faces.

A boy of five or six, naked except for a loincloth, his distinctive fair hair reaching to his skinny shoulders, when reunited with his birth mother, broke away and running between the forest of legs he slipped out of the meeting-house. Spotting the escapee, a soldier quickly slung his musket over his shoulder and gave chase. Ducking and weaving his way through the crowd, with the soldier in hot pursuit, the young boy suddenly felt a hand seize him by the arm and looking up he saw the face of Colonel Bouquet smiling benevolently down on him. With a nod to the pursuing soldier Colonel Bouquet watched for a moment as the child was led away back to the meeting-house. Turning away, his thoughts tinged with a slight feeling of unease, accompanied by Major Campbell, he continued on his way, moving almost unnoticed amongst the assembled throng of people, their clamorous voices ringing in his ears.

Reining in his horse the express-rider, the sleeve of his uniform now boasting a corporal's chevron, slipped down from the saddle and pleased to have his feet back on firm ground again, he walked purposefully through the rows of tents towards the meeting-house. Catching sight of Colonel Bouquet among the crowd, he shouldered his way through the crush of people until he was by his side, then with a quick salute he removed a despatch from his pouch and handed it over to the officer.

'A despatch from Fort Bedford sir.'

Taking the folded paper, sealed with a red blob of wax from him, Colonel Bouquet returned the express-riders salute and turning to Major Campbell, with the offending document held aloft, he remarked in a slightly amused manner.

'Another of Ourray's infernal letters. I swear the man has ink in his veins for he is forever putting pen to paper at the least provocation and on occasion, for no more reason than to inform me of events which are of no interest or importance whatsoever.'

Waiting until the two officers had disappeared into the throng of people gathered around the meeting-house, the express-rider turned away and in doing so, his gaze fell on a woman and a young girl standing like two lost souls on the fringe of the crowd their faces etched with despair. Wearing the same clothes, albeit now stained and soiled, as before, he recognised them immediately and without a moment's hesitation he made his way purposefully towards them.

The woman saw him first, her hand instinctively flying to her mouth, suppressing the cry of joy before it could escape her lips. Then the young girl, her golden curls matted and tangled, saw him too and her face lit up. The soldier she remembered seeing sitting astride his wonderful bay horse, was walking towards her and he was smiling.

Looking on from the fringe of the crowd, Adam witnessed their reunion with a pang of regret. Just for a moment he had dared to believe that the woman might be Esther. Disappointed, he turned away and drawn by the sound of voices carried on the breeze blowing up from the river and catching sight of more canoes arriving with their cargo of prisoners, he made his way down the slope towards the grassy bank, his hopes of finding Esther renewed.

Content that his demands for the release of their prisoners was being adhered to by the Indians and sorely in need of a moment's privacy, Colonel Bouquet moved away from the confines of the meeting-house. Passing by a small group of captives flanked by stoic warriors, his attention was caught by a settler woman kneeling before a young girl whom she clearly believed to be her long-lost daughter, carried off years earlier by the Indians when she was just an infant. Intrigued, Colonel Bouquet walked over and stood beside her. Sensing his presence, clearly distraught that the child had no recollection of her, the woman looked up at him, with tears running down her face.

'She doesn't know me.'

Gazing across at the young girl, who looked for all the world like an Indian child, tempering his words with a sympathetic tone Colonel Bouquet asked the woman.

'Forgive me but can you be sure that this child is your own?'

Horrified by his assertion the woman shouted back at him. 'I'm as sure as I breathe that this child is the very one as sat on my knee while I sung a lullaby to send her to sleep, I can be sure of that much.' Wiping at the tears streaming down her cheeks, she went on, 'she is my own darling daughter and she has forgotten me.'

Touched by her response, Colonel Bouquet leaned down and whispered quietly.

'Sing the song that you used to sing to her when she was a child.'

Bemused for a moment by his words, the woman stared back at him for a moment and then turning to face the young girl she began singing the words of a long forgotten lullaby. Immediately the young girl's face lit up as the words awakened dormant memories in her and with a joyful cry she flung herself into her mother's arms.

Dejected by his fruitless search of the new arrivals, Adam trudged back up the slope towards the row of rustic buildings where he and his father had been given temporary lodgings, having declared the loss of Adam's intended bride as a reason for their presence. With his mind on other things, it was purely by chance that Adam witnessed the arrival of Captain Bassett and his detachment of soldiers making their way between the rows of tents. Something had caught his eye, or perhaps it was just fate being kind but it was then that he saw her, his Esther, seated on the back of the pack-horse and his heart leapt. Elated beyond reason, barging his way through the crowd of people, he ran towards her. But before he had taken a dozen steps, a heavy hand took him by the shoulder and stopped him in his tracks.

Turning to see who had impeded his progress, Adam found himself stared into the eyes of his father. With a joyful cry he called out.

'Pa it's Esther, I've found her.' then pointing with his arm. 'Look there do you see her?'

With little conviction, Samuel looked towards were his son was pointing only to see that the lad was right, it was her. Despite the manner in which she was dressed and the different look to her hair, her face was unmistakable. But then his eyes found the infant clutched to her breast and his expression hardened. When he spoke his words carried a hard edge.

'Best we don't make ourselves known to her just yet.'

In a flash the smile was wiped from Adam's face.

'But Pa.'

Turning on him, Samuel spat out.

'Do as I say now.'

Consumed with disappointment, Adam dropped his head and without questioning his father's reason, obediently he turned and walked away. Following a step behind him, speaking his thoughts in a voice only he could hear, Samuel whispered aloud.

'The wolf may yet come seeking his cub.'

Having been exiled in the woods for days while the victorious soldiers searched the surrounding Indian villages, Shingas wolfed down the hot meal, placing the empty bowl on the cot beside him once he had scraped it clean. As he did so the old squaw entered his apartment carrying a large pot of freshly heated water which she set down at his feet. With her heart full of hope that Shingas would be successful in finding Esther and her infant, she had decided against revealing Meeataho's part in their abduction, content for the moment to delay her revenge on the young squaw for her treachery until after her family were restored to her. Leaving Shingas to his ablutions, without a word, she scooped up the empty bowl and left. Reaching into his carry-all Shingas removed a small earthenware jar containing a pale coloured paste. Dipping two fingers into it, he began working the substance into his face, smearing the carefully applied design of his war-paint until it resembled an artist's palette. Satisfied, he then soaked a cloth in the pot of steaming water and began washing all traces of the paint from his face. With all evidence of war removed from his features, Shingas picked up his musket and left his small room. The English redcoats had stolen his family, now he would take them back.

Seated at the entrance of the makeshift building to which she had been assigned, with the infant feeding contentedly at her breast, Esther was thankful for what little breeze there was. Behind her other women, some with babies and young children, lay stretched out on straw mattresses, some of them asleep, others merely seeking some shade. Looking out on the sea of activity before her, Esther caught sight of the young fair haired boy she had seen running away. Restored to his family and now clothed in a shirt and breeches, she watched him struggling as they attempted to put a pair of shoes on his feet. Overcome by a sudden pang of sadness Esther looked away and it was then that she saw him, standing as bold as a lion not twenty paces away his eyes fixed on her in an unblinking stare. Overwhelmed by a flood of emotions, yet strangely not afraid, Esther stared back at Shingas, watching as he walked brazenly towards her.

Suddenly a soldier appeared and seeing Shingas he stepped forward and blocked his path. Posted as a sentry at the end of each building, with his musket held across his chest, its naked bayonet a warning of intent, the soldier barked out.

'Halt!'

Eyeing the sentry with a mixture of hatred and disdain, Shingas instinctively reached for the tomahawk hanging from his belt. Threatened by the gesture, the sentry took a step backwards and levelling his bayonet at Shingas' chest he bellowed out.

'Corporal of the guard.'

Freeing the tomahawk from his belt Shingas caught sight of a group of armed soldiers as they rounded the corner of the building and made their way towards him. With his intentions foiled and not wishing to find himself in chains, Shingas turned on his heels and quickly strode away, pushing through the throng of people and losing himself among the crowd of warriors standing outside the meeting-house.

With a look of triumph Samuel plunged into the crowd after him, with Adam following close behind him like a faithful hound. Earlier, Samuel had seen where they had taken Esther and her baby and more vigilant than any sentry he had kept watch on them, silently praying that, if he were alive, that the one who had planted his seed in her would seek her out. Now his hopes and prayers were realised and with the spectre of his all-consuming hatred given substance, he would exact his revenge.

With all hope of taking back what was his gone, Shingas left the open meadow and the unfolding pageant of humanity being played out on its grassy stage and slipped away into the surrounding forest, loping through the crowded trees, and welcoming the cloak of anonymity they threw over him. Within minutes he knew he was being followed, the noise of his pursuer's heavy footfall easily discernible in the infinite silence of the woods. Unsuspecting, Samuel and Adam followed his trail like faithful bloodhounds on a scent, Samuel gulping in lungfuls of air as their quarry led them deeper into the forest. Without caring whether or not their presence was known, sensing fatigue seeping into his legs, Samuel lengthened his stride and began closing the gap between himself and the person he was determined to kill.

With his trap sprung and with less than a hundred paces between them, suddenly without warning, Shingas stopped and turned to face the two who were pursuing him, recognising them instantly. Hardly daring to believe his good fortune, with a shout of triumph, Samuel threw up his musket and with his heart beating like a drum inside his heaving chest he took aim, secretly praying as he did, that the musket ball would not kill its intended victim so that he could finish him slowly with the knife. But even as his finger came to rest on the trigger, Cattawa's tomahawk was already flying through the air towards him. Turning end over end, the sound of its whirling flight was like the wing-beat of a thousand hummingbirds, falling silent when, with a sickening thud its steel head embedded itself in the middle of Samuel's back and severed his spine. Pitched forward by the impact, compelled by hatred, with his dying reflex, Samuel squeezed the trigger, mercifully never to know that his messenger of death was to fly harmlessly above Shingas' head.

Shrieking his war-cry Cattawa leapt out from hiding and pulling his scalping knife from his belt he ran towards Samuel's prostrate body. Dropping onto his knees beside it, he reached out and seized his victim's scalp. But before the blade could slice into Samuel's scalp, with an enraged roar, Adam fell on him and fuelled by the surge of adrenalin coursing through his veins, he lifted the startled warrior into the air as though he weighed less than a pillow and like a petulant child tossing a doll from its pram, he hurled him onto the ground a dozen yards away. Drained, Adam fell down onto his knees beside the body of his father and oblivious to the dark stain ebbing out from deep wound in his back, in a singular act of devotion he began stroking his hair.

With his face contorted with hatred, Cattawa climbed to his feet and with his knife raised to strike, he rushed towards Adam. Instantly Shingas interposed himself between them, the gesture alone telling the angry warrior that this one was to be spared. Reluctantly Cattawa sheathed his knife and disgruntled he stepped away, watching in sullen silence as the other members of the small war-party gathered in a circle around Adam, looking down on him like a crowd of curious children. Consumed with grief Adam gazed imploringly up into their warlike faces and with tears spilling from his eyes, he began rocking gently back and forth, moaning like a tormented soul through half open lips. After a few moments, one of the warriors, obviously touched by Adam's agonising lamentations, reached down and took hold of him by the hand. Pulling Adam to his feet, with the other warriors gathered around him like a protective cloak, he lead the last of Samuel's sons away into the forest like a lost child.

CHAPTER FIFTEEN

EIGHT OPEN WAGONS, each drawn by a pair of oxen stood in line at the edge of the meadow. Their drivers, whips in hand, waiting patiently as the last of the women and children, unclaimed by neither husband nor family, climbed aboard in readiness for their journey back to the settlements. Gathered around them a jostling crowd of squaws, unrestrained in their display of sorrow at being parted from their adopted daughter-in-laws and children whom they had taken as their own, displayed their affection by furnishing them with food and blankets for the journey.

Seated in the lead wagon, Esther looked down on the distraught women with uncertain emotions. Suddenly the baby began to cry, it was hungry again. Welcoming the distraction, Esther unbuttoned the front of her new blue linen dress with its decorative patterns stitched into the neck and cuffs. The dress had been a gift from a kindly settler's wife. She would have no use for it she had cried when pressing it into Esther's hands. Telling how she and her husband had come in search of their long lost daughter but that their quest had been in vain and although begged by others not to give up hope, both, she said, were resigned to never having her returned to them.

With thundering hooves a young officer, resplendent in his scarlet jacket and tricorn hat rode up and bringing his lively mount under control, he shouted an order to the dozen or so soldiers standing a little way off in the shade of some trees. Obediently, they shouldered their muskets and made their way across to the wagons and pushing their way through the throng of squaws, they took up their station along each side of the small convoy. With the last woman and child safely aboard, accompanied by the crack of whips, the line of wagons lumbered forward towards the encircling forest.

Thanks in part to the rugged track, cleared so recently by the sweat and toil of Colonel Bouquet's axemen, the teams of oxen, with the young officer riding ahead of them, hauled the wagons along at a steady pace. Slogging along beside them, his escort of soldiers were already cursing the cloying heat. Seated up in the jolting carts, for the most part the women and children endured their bumpy journey in silence, some content to doze while others, especially those with babes and young children born to them in captivity, reflected on what might await them on their return to civilisation.

With the baby asleep in her arms these thoughts were also uppermost in Esther's mind. With no knowledge of the events that had unfolded before her abduction and up until as recently as two days ago, all she could focus her thoughts on, was the inevitable reunion with Samuel and Adam and what bearing her capture and the birth of a child would have on its outcome.

Her thoughts were interrupted by a chorus of shrieks from the wagon ahead of her, when one of its wheels struck the protruding stump of a tree, dislodging it from its axle and almost pitching its terrified occupants out.

Cursing aloud at his bad luck, the driver climbed down from his seat and calling out to a pair of gawking soldiers to lend a him a hand, he began helping his passengers down from their precarious perch.

With the wagon emptied of its human cargo, the driver removed a stout pole from the bed of the wagon and thrust it under the axle. Calling for another driver to help him, with knees bent, the two men set the pole on their shoulder and with a third driver standing ready with the wheel, they attempted to lift the tilted wagon but without success. Riding back along the convoy and seeing the two drivers struggling in vain to raise the wagon, the young officer shouted out angrily to a group of soldiers standing idly by.

'You men there lend a hand. Lively now!'

Grumbling under their breath the soldiers stacked their muskets and doing little to disguise their reluctance, they sauntered over to give assistance.

Standing among the group of women and children who had been helped down from the tilting wagon, the young fair haired boy cast a surreptitious look at the people around him. Seeing that all of them, including the escorting soldiers, were preoccupied by the efforts to restore the wheel to its axle, unnoticed, he backed away towards the wall of trees lining the track and with a last furtive look, he ducked under their outstretched branches and slipped away unseen into the forest.

Exhilarated and panting for breath, the runaway boy burst into the small forest clearing closely followed by three Indian boys of about the same age. United with his boyhood friends, he immediately began stripping off the clothes he had been forced to wear and throwing them onto the ground. Last to come off where his hated shoes and these he tossed high into the treetops, watching with great delight as their laces caught on a branch, leaving them hanging there like bizarre Christmas decorations. Whooping with joy at his transformation, the three Indian boys raced away into the forest. Naked and grinning like the proverbial Cheshire cat, the runaway turned to follow them. As he did so, he caught sight of Shingas standing among the trees on the far side of the clearing watching him, his cruel features transformed by the rarest of smiles. Hesitating for a moment, the runaway suddenly let out a defiant yell and turning away, with his pale backside flashing like the flag of a fleeing deer, he dashed off into the dark woods.

With dusk approaching and aware of how wearying the day's journey had been for his charges, the young officer called a halt for the night and after pulling the wagons off the track, he ordered the drivers to draw them up into a defensive square. Leaving the teamsters to attend to the needs of their oxen, he then set his men to making camp with instructions that a fire should be lit as a matter of urgency and a hot meal prepared. Whether by design or forgetfulness, it turned out that no tents had been loaded with the provisions but instead a good supply of blankets. However with little need for privacy and nothing to fear from the weather, except a warm night, the oversight was quickly forgotten by all.

As darkness fell like a cloak over the camp, with everyone fed and the young children settled for the night, most of the returnees took to their beds, almost all choosing to sleep under the wagons. The handful who were left, including Esther, stretched out their blankets on the ground, far happier to sleep out in the open. After setting a rota for sentry duty among his men, the young officer took a leaf from the drivers' book and climbing into the back of one of the wagons, he laid out his blanket on its wooden boards. He expected little trouble from any savages who might be skulking in the woods, he doubted any would dare attack the Kings soldiers, no matter how small in number especially given the severity with which Colonel Bouquet had treated them and the fearful reprisal they might expect should they misbehave. So, content that he had carried out his duty and with a sentry posted on the camps perimeter and another guarding the oxen, with his saddle as a pillow, he stretched out on the hard boards and with a good meal inside him, he was quickly asleep.

Stifling a yawn, the young soldier leaned his back against the scaly bark of the giant Hemlock and stared up at the sky, its inky blackness home to a million stars, twinkling above him like a swarm of heavenly fireflies. Captivated by the scene, his thoughts turned to the young girl he had become acquainted with during his two days spent at Fort Bedford. Pretty as a picture she was, far too pretty for the likes of him he had told himself, with her slender figure and eyes so deep and blue a person could drown in them. But mostly it was her lips that he remembered; rich and inviting like ripe cherries. Although he had never kissed a girl before, the thought of pressing his lips to hers made him feel quite dizzy. There were others of course who had their eye on her, older soldiers mostly, who sought her attention with their winks and salacious remarks. But it seemed his shyness endeared him to her and to his great surprise and joy, he was the one she had smiled at.

Immersed in a flood of memories, resting his musket between his legs, the young sentry reached into a pocket of his uniform and removed a small lace handkerchief. Holding it to his nose the scent of her perfume conjured up the moment when, with a tear in her eye, she had pressed it into his hand as they marched away down the narrow street, waving until he was out of sight.

With the handkerchief still pressed to his nose and alive to the prospect of seeing her again in a few days' time, the young soldier's eyes widened in disbelief when, as if by magic, Shingas appeared before him like some terrifying apparition. Staring into the sentry's startled face, Shingas reached out and clamping a hand over the young soldier's half open mouth, he drove the blade of his knife through the coarse material of his uniform and deep into his heart. Pressing him back against the tree until the convulsions stopped and his life had ebbed away, Shingas lowered the lifeless body to the ground,

Pulling his knife from the soldier's chest, Shingas wiped the blade clean, and silent as a shadow he moved unheard and unseen into the camp.

He quickly found Esther laying stretched out not far from the flickering remains of the fire with the infant close beside her. Partly covered by a blanket, both of them were lost in sleep. Bending down, in one fluid movement Shingas leaned forward and reaching out, he scooped the infant up into his arms. Esther never knew what made her reach out her hand. Some instinct perhaps? Some tiny warning voice inside her head? Whatever it was she was instantly awake, staring at the empty space on the blanket where her child had lain. Then, with the scream ready to escape from her mouth she saw him sitting opposite her, cross-legged on the ground, the child cradled in his arms. Half afraid, half relieved, unsure of what she should do, Esther stared at him. His face, illuminated by the soft glow from the dying fire, was as enigmatic as always and yet whether it was due to the absence of war-paint but she detected a softness to his features..

As if to confirm her feelings, unexpectedly and without uttering a word, Shingas suddenly held out his arms and offered the infant to her. Staring into his jet black eyes, Esther's took the baby from him and hugged it protectively to her breast. Expressionless, Shingas stood up and turning his back on them, his head held high, he slowly walked away into the darkness.

With a thousand thoughts flashing through her brain, Esther stared after him. Then with unshakable clarity she knew instinctively what she must do and leaping to her feet she hurried after him, weaving her way among the sleeping bodies, the infant clutched tightly in her arms.

In truth she could have stayed. She could have allowed herself to be repatriated to the settlements, with every chance that she would be claimed once more by Farmer Endicote. But what could she expect from him now except a return to a life of servitude, for with Saul dead he would have no need of her as a wife for Adam. What concerned her most though was the safety of her son. His very sight would be a constant reminder to the bereaved farmer of those who had murdered his family and she shuddered to think what he might do to him when the flames of vengeance eventually consumed him as they surely would.

Compelling though this was, if she was honest with herself, the real reason for her decision to turn her back on her past life and return to live amongst the Seneca was more deep rooted and personal. Condemned to a life of servitude from the age of sixteen, when her father, gripped in the jaws of depression's black dog, had put a pistol to his head and blown out his brains. She had been passed like a chattel from employer to employer until her indenture was eventually purchased by Samuel Endicote.

Living among the Seneca and no longer seen by them as a captive, she had found a freedom of sorts, a freedom she was loath to give up. She had also become part of a family again. She had a child, she had a husband and while it was true that he was a savage, she had glimpsed beneath his stern exterior and found a kind and loving heart. But the real act of persuasion was the fact that he had not just taken his son and disappeared with him into the night but that he had given him back to her and allowed her to choose their destiny. It was this simple truth which now bound her to him. Bound her as surely as if a vicar had stood over them and in the presence of God had pronounced them husband and wife.

Silently, Shingas and Esther passed the young sentry slumped at the foot of the tree with the young girl's favour still gripped in his hand, and together they moved away towards the serried ranks of trees, and in the space of a heartbeat they became moon-shadows and disappeared from sight in the gloomy darkness of the forest.

APPENDIX

I N AN EFFORT to ensure historical authenticity I have included extracts from the original documents held in the archives of the Pennsylvania Gazette at Harrisburg PA and the London Magazine for 1763. These include the letter from Captain Ecuyer to Captain Ourry and correspondence between Sir Jeffrey Amherst and Colonel Bouquet prior to and at the conclusion of the battle of Bushy Run.

Extracts of the speech by the Delaware chief Turtle Heart and Colonel Bouquet's response during the conference on the banks of the Muskingum River have been taken from Colonel Bouquet's official journals housed in the archives of the Pennsylvania Gazette.

This content was kindly provided by
Accessible Archives Inc.
on-line databases.

ABOUT THE AUTHOR

BARRY COLE WAS born in Yorkshire but spent much of his life in Bedfordshire. He served as a regular soldier and after leaving the army he began contributing stories and articles to two Native American Charities monthly magazines. Since then he has written several feature length screenplays and a children's book entitled The Time Bandit. Shingas is his first novel. He now lives on a narrow boat on the Grand Union canal in Northamptonshire.

Made in the USA
Monee, IL
14 April 2020